C000062479

SEAL'S SEDUCTION

TAKE NO PRISONERS BOOK #6

ELLE JAMES

TWISTED PAGE INC

SEAL'S SEDUCTION

TAKE NO PRISONERS BOOK #6

New York Times & *USA Today*
Bestselling Author

ELLE JAMES

Ebook ISBN: 978-1-62695-019-1

Print ISBN: 978-1-62695-020-7

FROM THE AUTHOR

This book is dedicated to the families of our service members who take care of everything while their soldier, sailor, airman or marine is away. They're the ones who keep the home fires burning and are there when these heroes come home. As an Air Force brat, I remember the many times my father deployed to the other side of the planet. He'd be gone for six months to a year at a time. My mother held down the fort with four children and welcomed my father home each time with open arms. Back then, we didn't have the ability to log onto the Internet and talk with my father. We didn't even have the ability to pick up a telephone and talk to him. I have memories of crying in the night because I couldn't remember my father's face. The joy we experienced upon his return was priceless.

Escape with...
Elle James
aka Myla Jackson

AUTHOR'S NOTE

Enjoy other military books by Elle James

Visit ellejames.com for more titles and release dates
For hot cowboys, visit her alter ego Myla Jackson at
mylajackson.com
and join Elle James and Myla Jackson's Newsletter at
Newsletter

1

Two miles away from its target location, the Black Hawk helicopter slowed and hovered thirty feet off the ground. The whirling blades stirred the sultry night heat of Somalia.

Dustin Ford, nicknamed Dustman by his team, was first out, fast-roping to the ground. As soon as he hit the dirt, he ran to the two o'clock position to establish his section of the perimeter, his M4A1 aimed out into the dry foliage, his night vision goggles in place as he scanned for any heat signatures in the area.

The satellite images had pinpointed the Somali rebel camp at two miles to the south of where they'd landed. Even before the last man hit the ground, Dustin took point, moving quietly through the night.

Orders from above were to neutralize the rebels and rescue the American aid workers who had been held captive in an attempt to extort money from the U.S. government for their return.

With Irish on his right, Gator on his left and Tuck at his back, he'd be first to make contact. Intel estimated twenty rebel fighters, armed with whatever weapons they had collected. They would put up a fierce resistance...if the SEAL team lost the element of surprise early on. But Dustin's team was trained to get in and get out with minimal effort and loss of American lives.

As they neared the camp, Dustin could make out three blurry green heat signatures of sentries spread out fifty feet apart on the perimeter of the camp. He figured there were more on the other side.

Big Bird, Fish, Swede, Nacho and Rider fanned out to either side. While they moved into place to take out the sentries farther away, Dustin and his crew held fast, waiting for their cue to move in and silently dispatch the camp guards.

"In position," Big Bird said in Dustin's ear. Knives drawn, the team moved in. Before the guards knew what hit them, they were dispatched and lying silently in the dirt, their terrorist days done.

A sharp report of gunfire pierced the silence. A shout rose from one of the five tents, and terrorists wielding semi-automatic rifles and AK-47s rushed out of four of the five tents.

The SEAL team had the advantage of night vision goggles. One by one, they picked off the terrorists until the last one fell.

Dustin ducked low and ran toward the one tent no gunmen had emerged from. Other members of his team rushed the other tents and cleared them. More gunfire erupted and the usual confusion of battle ensued.

As he neared the exterior, Dustin shouted in Arabic for anyone inside the tent to come out. At first, he didn't hear anything. Then quiet sobbing came from inside. Dustin nodded to Gator, the big Cajun, who stood close to the entrance of the tent, while Dustin rounded to the rear.

When Gator repeated the Arabic command, Dustin drove his knife into the canvas and ripped an opening of his own.

A woman's scream filled the air. A dark-skinned Somali, his eyes rounded, held the American woman with a knife to her throat. He shouted in Arabic, "I will kill her."

Dustin eased forward, his hands out to the side, speaking in Arabic, "Put the knife down and we will let you live." While he had the Somali's attention, Gator slipped through the front flap and attacked the man from behind.

The terrorist fell forward, dead with a knife to the base of his skull, severing his brain stem.

The woman he'd held captive scrambled through the opening, her eyes wide, sobs shaking her body.

Dustin grabbed her and held her tight. For a woman in her late fifties, she fought like a wildcat, kicking and screaming, her fingernails slashing at his face.

"Martha!" he said, his voice stern, breaking through her crazed attempt at escape. "I'm an American, here to take you home."

He had to repeat himself several times before he got through to her and she sagged against him, her body spent, her sobs fading to silent tears. She clung to him for a moment then pushed away. "John." She dropped to the floor beside the man lying on a grass mat, his eyes closed.

"Is he dead?" Gator asked.

Dustin squatted beside the man and pressed two fingers to the base of his throat. A weak, but steady pulse pushed back against his fingertips. "He's alive, but in bad shape. You take Martha. I'll get John."

Martha stumbled to her feet, swayed and would have fallen if Gator hadn't been there to scoop her up in his arms.

Dustin bent toward John and draped his body over his shoulder, then stood and exited through the front flap, held open by Irish.

"Need a hand?" Irish asked.

"I've got him."

The whop-whop of rotor blades filled the air. The sting of dust and flying debris whipped up into Dustin's face as he hurried toward the Black Hawk, depositing his charge on the floor of the craft. Fish bent over the man and went to work establishing an IV drip. Both John and Martha were suffering from severe dehydration and malnutrition from the month of captivity they'd endured with the Somali rebels, but they'd live, now that they were on their way home to the States.

Dustin glanced around at his teammates. All were present and accounted for. Mission accomplished, with no casualties except for those terrorists who would never terrorize another soul.

After they boarded the C-130 to take them home, Tuck reported in with headquarters back in Little Creek, Virginia. When he came back to check on the team, he pulled Dustin aside. "As soon as we get back, you're to pack up and head to Texas."

Dustin's stomach took a dive to his kneecaps. "Why? What happened?"

"Your father had a heart attack. You'll be on emergency leave for a couple weeks."

"JENNA TURNER, reporting live to you from a normally quiet street on the south side of Waco." Jenna faced the camera, holding the microphone in front of her mouth. Her pulse pounded and her hand shook slightly, but she forced herself to be calm and report the news as unbiased and composed as she could. "It's been four hours since Frank Mitchell barricaded himself in his mother's home, threatening to kill the elderly woman if anyone tried to come in after him." Toby, her cousin and cameraman, moved in a slow arc, recording behind her the modest white clapboard house with the old fashioned, metal awnings and peeling paint.

Jenna continued her monologue, "Our sources tell us Mitchell is wanted on several counts of armed robbery, assault, selling methamphetamines and resisting arrest. He could be under the influence of the drugs he deals and is considered a threat to his elderly parent."

The camera angled back toward her. "The Waco PD hostage negotiator has been on scene from the beginning, but nothing has changed in the past four hours." Except the fact her feet were killing her in her high-heeled boots, and she hadn't made it to a bathroom in hours. She regretted downing the fully leaded—sugar and caffeine-loaded—Dr. Pepper over an hour ago. If things didn't get hopping soon, she'd knock on a neighbor's door and ask to use their facilities.

"Jenna! Check it out. The SWAT team is headed in," Toby called out from behind the camera. He aimed his lens at the black armored van pulled to a stop two houses down from where Mitchell holed up. Men poured out, dressed in black uniforms, with olive drab bulletproof vests buckled in place over their chests.

Jenna's pulse leaped. Holy shit, this was it! This was her big chance to make it onto the national news. Alongside raging fires sweeping across California and hurricanes in the gulf, hostage situations ranked right up there and she was here, on the scene, camera ready. She held the microphone away from her mouth and whispered loud enough Toby could hear, "Are you getting this?"

"Damn right I am."

"We're here at the scene," Jenna said into the microphone. "The SWAT team has arrived, and they're surrounding the house."

"Ma'am." A police officer blocked Jenna's view. "You'll have to back away from the house."

"But..." Jenna's pulse quickened and she stood on her toes to see past the policeman.

"I'm sorry. The chief insists all civilians remove themselves to a block away, in case shit hits the fan."

Members of the SWAT team took up positions around the house, poised to launch their attack and the big police officer had his hand in front of the damned camera.

Jenna dug her heels into the pavement. "I'm a reporter." She dug her press identification card out of her pocket and waved it in his face. "I have a right to be here."

The officer shook his head and spread his arms wide as if he would herd her away like a stray calf. "The chief said all civilians, including the press. It's for your own safety."

"What if I choose to accept the risk?"

"That doesn't mean squat to the chief. Off you go now, or I'll have to arrest you for interfering in a police operation."

"Damn!" This was her chance to show her boss at the station she could handle the intense and gritty situations.

Toby backed up, lowering his camera to catch what he could beneath the officer's arm. "Come on, Jenna. Let's do as the officer asks."

"But it's happening here and now. If we leave, we lose

this opportunity."

Toby hooked her arm and dragged her down the street. "It's okay. We'll get a shot at it again." He leaned close to her. "You're wasting time. Come on. I have another idea."

Biting down on her lip, Jenna allowed Toby to drag her down the street. As soon as the police officer turned his back, Toby snagged Jenna's arm and yanked her between two houses.

They backtracked to a deserted house catty-corner to the one under siege. Toby fished a metal file out of his front pocket and would have jammed it into the lock.

Jenna laid a hand on his arm and shook her head. "It's open." She gave the door a slight shove and it swung inward. The interior was empty, all furniture gone, and no drapes in the window. Old, broken, vinyl blinds hung in the windows, some open, others closed.

Toby gestured with his camera toward a staircase. "Ladies first."

Jenna scampered to the top and hurried for a front window, thanking her stars for her cousin's ingenuity. Now if they could keep from being arrested for breaking and entering, they might have a shot at catching the hostage crisis on video.

The little house had a single room at the top of the stairs, a loft with two gables protruding out over the roof. Jenna opened the cheap blinds and peered out.

For a moment she thought she might have missed the show. Nothing moved. She couldn't see the SWAT team and the police had all backed up, positioned behind the relative security of their patrol cars.

"I have a clear view from here," Toby called out. He'd parted the blinds over the gabled window and stuck his camera lens through the gap. Kneeling on the floor, he gazed into the viewfinder. "Nothing's happening."

"Do you think they're already inside?" Jenna asked.

"No. If they had made their move, the rest of the cops hanging around would be a little more agitated. Right now, the police are pointing their weapons at the house."

"Then let's do this." Her heart racing, Jenna switched on her microphone. "This is Jenna Turner, reporting from the scene of a hostage crisis in Waco. The SWAT team has arrived and is in position."

"There they go," Toby whispered, excitedly.

Jenna stared through the blinds as half a dozen SWAT team policemen stormed through the front door.

Though muffled by the glass in the windows, the distinct pop-pop sound of gunfire could be heard, followed by shouts. A window exploded near the front of the house and a man Jenna assumed was Mitchell fell out on the ground and rolled to his feet, pistol in both hands.

"He's on the ground." Jenna jerked the blinds up to better see what was going on.

The officers behind their vehicles opened fire, but not before Mitchell let loose a round of bullets, some hitting the police cars.

Her voice shaking, Jenna spoke into her mic, "Mitchell is out of the house, firing at the police behind the barricade. He's been hit! But he's not going down without a fight."

As the bullets slammed into the man, he jerked, his hands rising, the guns with them. He dropped to his knees, still firing, only this time into the air.

The plink of glass breaking was quickly followed by a stinging sensation against her right temple. "Ouch." Jenna ducked to the side, refusing to look away from the scene unfolding.

Then it was over. Mitchell collapsed onto the front lawn of his mother's house and lay still.

The SWAT team emerged. One man had his arm around an old woman, helping her through the door and out into the open, shielding her from the sight of her son lying on the ground.

"Show's over. Let's transmit this to the station." Toby straightened and glanced her way, his brow furrowing. "Jenna, what the hell?"

She dragged her gaze from what was going on below and glanced at Toby. "What?"

"Your face is bleeding."

She raised her hand to where she could feel a slight stinging sensation and encountered warm wetness. "What's this?"

"Sweetheart, it's blood."

Jenna glanced at her fingers, covered in her own blood. Her knees weakened, and her head spun. "I think I've been shot."

Then the bright Texas sun outside blinked out.

2

ustin arrived in Dallas a day later, having slept maybe two hours on the plane, worry making his mind race ahead. He rented a truck, unwilling to burden his family further with picking him up at the airport. His father was scheduled for emergency surgery that day.

Since he'd landed in Dallas, he'd been in contact with his older brother Adam. His mother was with his father in pre-op. All was as well as could be expected until their father came out of surgery. Houston, his younger brother was on his way in from black ops training with the U.S. Army's Delta Force. Adam expected him to arrive any moment.

By the time Dustin reached the hospital in Waco, his internal engine was running on fumes. Six cups of coffee had him so jittery he could barely sit still. He hadn't felt that level of exhaustion since BUD/s training when he became a SEAL. Lack of sleep and the emotional drain of knowing his father might die had taken its toll.

Once he parked, he dropped to the ground, his legs shaky from jet lag. He dragged in a deep breath and let it out slowly, then jogged to the entrance of the hospital and burst through the door.

With the sun glaring off the glass, he didn't see what was behind it until he slammed into a young auburn-haired woman with a bandage around her forehead, rising out of a wheelchair. He dug his boots into the smooth tile floor, but not soon enough to halt his forward momentum. Dustin barreled into the young woman, grabbed her around the middle, threw himself over onto his back and landed hard on the ground, the woman landing on top of him, forcing the air from his lungs.

"What the hell?" The female pushed against his chest and stared down at him, her green eyes shooting flames. "Of all the idiotic, stupid things to do, plowing into a hospital full of sick and injured tops the charts."

Still fighting for his breath, Dustin opened his mouth but nothing came out. He sucked in a ragged breath, his mind clearing about the same time as recognition dawned. "Jenna?" he wheezed.

The woman's skillfully arched brows puckered, and then a smile lit her face. "Dustin?"

She rolled to the side and air flowed into Dustin's lungs.

Her joyous smile crashed into a deep frown. "Holy hell, can't you enter a building like everyone else?"

"I'm sorry. I didn't see you." Dustin sat up, grabbed her arms and stared into her face, memories of the woman crashing in around him. "Are you okay?" God, she was even more beautiful than when he'd left for Navy Basic Training a decade ago. He nodded toward the white gauze wrapped around her head. "Why are you wearing that?"

The bandage slipped loose and dropped down over one of her eyes. "Damn." She unwound the binding from her head and wadded it into her fist. "I told them this was too much." A butterfly bandage stretched over a cut on her temple, holding the edges of skin together.

His grip tightened. "What happened to your forehead?"

She snorted, shook free from his hold and pointed at the injury. "This little thing?"

"Don't let her fool you. It's a gunshot wound." A tall, lanky man with a baby face extended his hand to Jenna. "Need a hand up?"

Jenna placed her hand in his and let him draw her to her feet, her color rising in her cheeks. "It didn't hurt."

"Yeah, but had it hit one inch over, you wouldn't be falling all over a man in the hospital lobby. You'd be stretched out on a table in the morgue."

Jenna's face blanched.

"Damn, Jenna." Dustin pushed to his feet. "What happened?"

"Nothing," Jenna smoothed her hair back from her

face, like she did when she was avoiding an answer. She winced when her hand brushed over the bandage.

The lanky dude answered, "We were reporting on a hostage situation when the gunman started shooting at everything. After the gunman was hit by the SWAT team, his shots went wild. One nicked my girl, here."

"Fuck." Dustin planted himself in front of her, cupped her chin and studied the injury, his hands tingling with the electricity that shot through him whenever he touched this woman. Even after ten years, she still made him crazy.

"The doctor said it shouldn't leave much of a scar." Jenna laughed shakily. "He glued it together, rather than stitching."

Dustin shook his head. "What have you been up to since I've been gone?"

Jenna pulled free of his grip, the color returning to her cheeks. Rubbing her hands over her arms, she tilted her chin. "I'm a freelance reporter for the local news station."

The young man behind her grinned. "Yeah, and she's good. Today's report ought to get us into the national news."

Dustin glared at the man who'd gone with Jenna into danger. "Who the hell are you?"

The young man's grin slipped. "Toby." His own eyes narrowed. "Who the hell are you?"

His chest swelling out, his back stiffening, Dustin answered, "Dustin Ford. Jenna's fiancé."

Toby's brows rose into the hair hanging down over his forehead. "Fiancé?" He glanced from Jenna to Dustin and back to Jenna. "Is there something you haven't told me?"

She shook her head. "Former fiancé. A million years ago." Jenna brushed her hands over her rumpled skirt suit. "We were teenagers in lust. Not a brain between the two of us. We're lucky we broke it off before we made the biggest mistake of our lives."

Dustin's chest tightened. Jenna had been the one to break it off, claiming she wanted to live before she settled down. Being married came with too much responsibility, too many strings attached. She wanted to see the world, to experience life.

That had been right after the Navy recruiter had contacted him with an offer to join the Navy and a shot at the Navy SEALs training.

He'd been ready to turn it down, head to college and married life with Jenna—until she'd handed him her engagement ring, telling him no thanks. In that moment, his heart had broken into a million pieces. He'd told her to sell the ring, keep it or throw it away. He had no use for it in the Navy. That had been the last time he'd seen her.

Until now.

Ten years older, and she still looked the same. Only better. Her curves had filled out and her face had lost its youthful roundness. Apparently, she was still the same Jenna, running headlong into trouble, just like she had in high school. But why was she still in Waco?

"Wait." That woman with the flashing green eyes bit on her lip and touched his arm. "Why are you here?"

Remembering his reason for coming to Waco in the first place, Dustin glanced at his watch. "My father had a heart attack. He's having surgery as we speak."

Jenna's fingers tightened on his arm. "I'm sorry to hear that. You should go to your family."

He nodded and took a step toward the elevators.

"Wait," Jenna's soft voice said behind him. "How long will you be in town?"

Dustin's heart skipped several beats. Why should he care? Jenna had dumped him all those years ago, and he thought he'd gotten over her. Seeing her again brought back too many good memories along with the bad. Did he really want to open that old wound again? He didn't dare look back. He took another step and threw over his shoulder. "I'll be around for at least a week, depending on how my dad does."

He didn't glance back until he reached the elevator. When he did, his heart flip-flopped when he remembered just how much it hurt to walk away from Jenna the first time.

Jenna tried hard not to watch as Dustin walked away, but her hungry gaze followed him, until he entered the elevator and caught her staring. Her stomach bunched and her eyes stung.

"Fiancé?" Toby gripped her elbow. "I never knew you were engaged."

"How could you? You were in grade school at the time."

"Damn, woman." Toby's head moved back and forth as he helped her through the door. "How'd you let that one get away?"

She shrugged. "He's not all that."

"He's big, he's rugged. From what Marcy said, women like a man who can sweep her off her feet."

And he'd certainly done that. "He nearly put me right back in the hospital," she muttered. But damn, he was even sexier than he'd been in high school. All those lovely muscles had stretched his T-shirt across his broad chest, and they'd been rock-solid beneath her hands. Her belly clenched and a wash of desire spread through her body. Damn, damn, damn. He still had that effect on her, even after ten years.

"So, what gives?" Toby persisted. "Why'd you let him go?"

"He didn't need a wife weighing him down when he was about to go through the hardest training in his life. The man's a Navy SEAL." She pushed through the door and out into the hot, Texas sunshine.

Toby followed. "Let me get this straight, you dumped him so he could train to be a SEAL?"

"Yeah, so?" She pressed gently against the butterfly bandage, sending a sharp pain across her forehead. It was nothing compared to the heartache she'd experienced when she'd sacrificed her engagement so that Dustin could follow his dream.

"My cousin could have been married to a Navy SEAL." Toby shook his head as he held the passenger door open to her SUV. "Talk about your missed opportunities. I thought most girls wanted to marry the strong alpha dudes."

She ignored the open door, rounded to the other side and slid into the driver's seat. "He wouldn't have been a Navy SEAL had we gotten married. He'd have stayed in Texas, gone to college and become something he hated, an accountant or a businessman to support me and the family we would have had."

Toby slid into the passenger seat and buckled his seatbelt. "Is that such a bad thing?"

"The key?" She held out her hand, delaying her answer. She'd wondered the same thing for the past ten years. If she hadn't broken their engagement, would they have been happy? Would they still be together? Or would Dustin have let his regret fester? They'd have had a couple of kids—a girl with Jenna's auburn hair, and a boy with Dustin's black hair and brown eyes—and about the time the seven-year-itch set in, they'd have divorced and the kids would be juggled between the two of them.

Toby handed her the car key, his brow wrinkling. "Are you sure you should be driving after suffering a head wound?"

"It was a scratch."

"Yeah, and then you were knocked off your feet."

"I can manage." She twisted the key in the ignition and drove out of the parking lot.

For the first block, Toby sat quietly in the seat beside her. Jenna breathed a sigh of relief. Hopefully he wouldn't continue to badger her about her former fiancé. After all, that was ten years ago. They'd been kids.

A traffic light turned red and Jenna slowed to a stop.

Toby turned to her and opened his mouth.

"You're not going to let this go, are you?"

He grinned. "I saw the sparks between the two of you."

"That was anger on my part for being bowled over by a Neanderthal."

A snort sounded beside her. "Yeah. And he couldn't stop putting his hands on you. And the way his nostrils flared when he did, was a dead giveaway." Toby raised his hands. "Just sayin'."

Jenna's heart fluttered and she shot a glance his way. "You think?" The words left her mouth before she could think through them.

"Ah!" Toby raised a single finger. "So, you still have feelings for the Neanderthal."

The light turned green.

Her cheeks heating, Jenna floored the accelerator. "Even if I did, he's only in town for a week then he's back to being a Navy SEAL, deployed all over the world. SEALs don't have a life outside of their work."

Toby stared forward for a few minutes.

Jenna remained tense, waiting for the next round of badgering. Was it too much to ask for him to drop the subject? Her body was on fire just thinking about Dustin.

All she wanted was to get back to her apartment, strip, shower and crawl into her bed with her vibrator. A little self-pleasure would be much more satisfying than opening her heart to a man who wouldn't be around next week.

"How long has it been since you've slept with a man?" Toby asked.

"Toby! You're my cousin! My younger cousin." She glared his way and turned onto the street leading to his apartment. "That's not the kind of question you ask your relative."

"Why not?" He raised his hands palms up. "Damn, Jenna. I'm trying to make a point. How long has it been since you...you know?"

"You know what?"

"Come on. Do you want me to spell it out?"

"Since I got laid?" Jenna couldn't believe the kid she used to babysit was asking her such personal questions. "I have sex." She squirmed in her seat. "Not that it's any of your business." She pulled into the parking lot at his apartment building.

Toby remained in his seat, his gaze locking with Jenna's. "With a man or with a vibrator?"

Cheeks flaming, Jenna huffed. "I'm not believing this conversation." She pointed to the door. "Get out."

"I take it you haven't gotten laid in a long time." He crossed his arms over his chest. "Ten years?"

Jenna opened her mouth to say no, but the lie stuck in her suddenly constricted throat.

Toby nodded. "Thought so."

"So, it doesn't mean anything other than I know how to make myself happy. Besides, women don't need sex like men do."

Toby snorted loudly. "Not according to Marcy. She wants it all the time. She's practically insatiable."

Jenna pressed her hands to her ears. "Too much information, Toby."

"The way I see it, you have a week to enjoy with an old flame. What's stopping you?"

"The man's father is in the hospital. He has other things on his mind besides a week-long orgy with the woman who dumped him."

"Doesn't hurt to ask." Toby pushed the door open and stepped out. He leaned down. "Think about it. You probably already are. Why else did you ask him how long he'd be in town?"

Jenna refused to look at her young relative, keeping her gaze pinned to the garbage bin at the end of the parking lot, her heart pounding so loud in her ears, she couldn't think straight.

"You work hard, Jenna," he said, his voice softening, "you deserve a little happiness. Even if it's only for a week. It might loosen up those creative juices and make you an even better reporter." Toby slammed the door and walked off. When he was a good three feet ahead of her SUV, he turned and winked.

"Yeah, right." Jenna shifted into reverse and swung her vehicle around. Then she floored the accelerator and the SUV leaped out into the street, nearly taking out a motorcyclist, ambling along at the posted speed limit.

"Damn!" Jenna slammed on her brakes and pulled herself together. This was the reason she would be smart not to start anything with Dustin Ford. The man made her entirely too crazy. She'd be a fool to get involved for only a week with the SEAL. It had taken every ounce of her resolve to break it off with the man the first go-around. And she hadn't had a steady boyfriend or dated anyone more than two times before she refused to see him again. All because Dustin Ford had set the bar for all other men and none had measured up.

As she drove the few blocks to her apartment, a thought wiggled its way past her defenses.

If she chose to seduce the SEAL, maybe she'd find him to be a complete bore now. They'd both matured since high school. If she slept with him, she might learn that he wasn't as good as she remembered and she could finally move on with her life without having Dustin in her head every time she kissed someone.

Her mind spun with the possibilities and her core tightened. Jenna pulled into her parking lot, a plan forming. No sooner did she slide the SUV into her reserved spot, then she shifted into reverse and headed to the nearest mall for the Victoria's Secret shop to stock up on pretty panties and bras. If she was going to do this, she might as well do it right. Out with the granny panties, in with thongs and demi-bras.

Here's to getting some and getting on with my life.

3

Dustin found Adam and Houston in the surgical waiting room with their mother. All three were on their feet, pacing in different directions. When they spied him, they converged.

"Dustin!" Adam, the oldest of his brothers with the signature broad shoulders, dark hair and brown eyes of the Ford men, reached him first and enveloped him in a bear hug that squeezed the air from his lungs. "I really didn't think you'd make it. I'm glad you came."

Houston stuck out his hand and gripped it in a bone-crunching shake, and then he pulled him into a bear hug equal to Adam's.

His little brother's long lanky body had filled out with hard muscles. "Good to see you, bro."

They parted and his mother moved in, her eyes filling with tears. She opened her arms and Dustin stepped into them. Jeannie Ford was a good foot shorter than her 'boys', but she had the biggest heart in the state of Texas. She'd raised them, loved them and looked after them until they'd all gone their separate ways, each choosing a different career path.

Adam was the only brother who'd stayed in Texas. He'd gone on to college, obtaining a degree in criminal justice, and gone to work for the Waco Police department. His skills with all forms of weapons and tactics landed him on the SWAT team.

Houston had enlisted into the Army, excelled in airborne training and gone on to join the elite Delta Force.

"I'm so glad you could make it," their mother said. "Your father didn't want us to tell you and Houston about his surgery. But we disregarded his wishes."

"I'm glad you did and that I was on the tail end of a mission, or they might not have been able to contact me." Dustin glanced toward the door. "Any word?"

"They took him back an hour ago. Depending on what they find and how extensive the damage is, it could take a while." His mother sighed, her gaze on the empty doorway as if she could see through the walls into the operating room. "I hope he's okay."

"Knowing Dad, he'll be harassing the doctors and nurses in no time."

His mother's laugh was more like a sob. "He hates being sick."

Dustin nodded, forcing a smile. "He'll be a helluva a patient."

His mother stood taller, her back stiffening. "He'll have to get over it. He's going to do exactly what they say and get better. I have too many years left on this earth and refuse to spend them without him."

Dustin's heart swelled with his love for his parents. "That's right. You better practice now telling him no. Otherwise, he'll be out chopping down trees, herding cattle or pounding fence posts into the ground before he has a chance to heal."

"I'm taking off the next couple weeks from the police department to help out at home," Adam said. "Fortunately, Dad's ranch hand is capable and ready to take on the full load until Dad is recovered enough to help."

Dustin's brows rose. "Dad has a ranch hand?"

"When all you boys moved out, he and I thought we could do it all with occasional temporary help. But the teenagers we hired never last long," his mother said. "When my horse threw me and I injured my back, your father finally gave in and hired a fulltime ranch hand, by the name of Carson Scott. Thank God."

His stomach sank and he gripped his mother's hands. "Mom, I didn't know you'd been thrown." He raked his gaze over his mother, noticing the wrinkles around her eyes had deepened. "You're okay?"

She laughed and pulled her hands from his. "That was ages ago. After a little physical therapy I was fine."

Dustin shot a narrow-eyed glance at Adam. "Why didn't I hear about this?"

"I tried calling you, but you'd been deployed. By the

time you got back, Mom was well on her way to recovery. Besides, what could you have done?"

"Did you know about this?" Dustin asked Houston.

Houston nodded. "Adam contacted me, but Mom insisted she was fine. I couldn't have come if I'd wanted to. I was stepping on the plane for a mission."

His mother held up her hands. "Now, you two stop worrying about me and your father. We're going to be just fine. You can't live your lives around ours. Poor Adam does enough of it for all three of you."

Guilt gnawed at Dustin's gut. "I should be here for you."

"You're a Navy SEAL, and Houston is part of Delta Force." She cupped Dustin and Houston's faces and smiled at them. "You do more for the good of our country, and I'm so very proud of my boys." She backed up, dropping her hands to her sides. "All of my boys." She reached for Adam's arm and hugged it. "Did you know Adam received a letter of commendation from the mayor of Waco for saving the lives of a woman and her baby being held captive by her ex-husband?"

Dustin shook his head. "I didn't know that." He didn't know a lot about his family. He'd been away so long, to various missions and training exercises, he hadn't kept in touch as much as he should have. Ten years in the Navy was a long time, especially when it was as a SEAL. He'd seen more battle than most seasoned soldiers and killed his share of the enemy. "Mom, maybe it's time for me to quit the Navy and come home."

"Oh, sweetheart, as long as you love what you do, keep doing it. We'll get along fine."

"Yeah, but I could find a job at something closer to home and be nearer in case something like this happens again."

His mother's lips pressed together. "Let's hope and pray nothing like this happens again. I'll admit, I never felt so helpless as when your father went down and I could do nothing."

Houston slipped an arm around his mother. "Dustin and I would quit the military tomorrow and come back home to help out."

"And your father would have a conniption. He's so proud of you three, he can't stop talking about you to his cronies at Casey's diner." Their mother patted Houston's arm. "I'm going to make a trip to the ladies' room. When I get back, I don't want to hear any more about you two quitting the military."

As soon as their mother left the waiting room, Dustin turned to Adam. "How bad is it? Do we need to come home for good?"

Houston stood beside Dustin.

Adam crossed his arms over his chest. "As long as I'm here, I've got it covered."

"Yeah, but that isn't fair to you, taking on the full responsibility of looking out for Mom and Dad."

"I'm happy here and doing what I love, chasing bad guys and helping in hostile situations. Besides, what would you two do if you came back to Waco?"

Dustin shoved a hand through his hair and shook his head. "I don't know. Join the police force, go back to college, something."

"And you'd hate it. You both thrive on action. Fitting into the slow pace of civilian life would kill you."

Houston nodded. "Every time I'm home on vacation, I'm itching to get back to my unit. Lazing around in the sunshine is only good for a couple days, a week max."

Dustin knew exactly what that felt like. Too many of his buddies who'd walked away from active duty had troubles assimilating into the civilian life. From being shot at, having rockets exploding around you and always having to look around corners for the enemy, they'd gone slowly crazy. He didn't want to turn out like that.

"A buddy of mine left the service last year and started his own private investigative and bodyguard service," Houston said. "If I leave the service anytime soon, I'd do that. I'd be using my combat training and skills as a marksman."

Dustin considered Houston's suggestion. "How much of a demand is there for that kind of thing?"

"More than you think," Adam said. "A man from Dallas approached me not too long ago about just such an organization. Wanted me to go to work for him."

"Why work for someone else," Dustin said. "Why not set up our own business?"

Adam snorted. "Do you have connections with people who have the money to afford such a business?"

He had a point. "I guess it would be good to let

someone else do the paperwork. I never was one for reports and finances."

"I'll see if I can find the man's card," Adam said.

In the meantime, Dustin walked over to the television and hit the on button. He hadn't seen a news report in the past week. For all he knew the Hutus and the Tutsis, Ugandan genocide, could be at it again, the Somali rebels could have completely overthrown the government and the Iranians could be lobbing nuclear bombs into Israel or vice versa.

The local station had a special report playing.

"We have this report from earlier this morning from our own reporter, Jenna Turner."

"What the..." Dustin turned up the volume.

Jenna stood with her back to a small cottage in a rundown neighborhood, a microphone held to her lips. God, she was gorgeous in her black skirt and kelly-green jacket, her auburn hair curling around her face.

She was saying something about a hostage situation and there were police cars between her and the white clapboard house.

A police officer approached her and forced her to move. The video cut and came back at an elevated vantage point, overlooking the same house and the SWAT team moving in on the house.

"I would have been there this morning, if I hadn't taken off today," Adam said, over Dustin's shoulder. "I'm surprised they let the reporter that close for so long. We usually keep civilians, even the news crews, far enough back from crisis situations. I'm surprised the chief let the Turner woman report that close."

"Hey, isn't that the girl you dated in high school?" Houston asked. "I remember you bringing her out to the ranch several times."

Dustin chuckled, while his gaze stayed glued on the screen. "Yeah, you were a pest, following us around. No matter what we did, we couldn't shake you."

Houston grinned. "I know, I caught you kissing her behind the barn a couple times."

The video continued with a bird's eye view of the house and the action surrounding it. A man fell out of a window and came up shooting, his weapons pointed at the police until he was shot in the chest. He jerked backward and continued to fire, this time, the guns were aimed every which way. All the while, Jenna ran a commentary, her voice rising, excited.

The sound of breaking glass cut her off, and she exclaimed, "Ouch!"

Dustin stepped closer to the television, wishing the camera would swing to the woman, but it didn't. A moment later, the gunman lay still on the ground and the video cut back to the anchorwoman in the news studio.

"Hey, Dustin, are you all right?"

"Damn." Now he knew why Jenna had come to the hospital. "Jenna was hit by one of those bullets."

"What?" Adam stared at Dustin. "How do you know?"

"I ran into Jenna in the hospital lobby on my way in. She had a bandage on her head from a gunshot wound."

"I swear that woman has a suicide wish. Every time we turn around, she's there. I think she has a relative on the force, or she's listening in on a police scanner. She's been at every major police or SWAT team event—sometimes before the police get there."

"She always liked more adventurous pursuits," he muttered.

"The local station usually has her do the social reports, weddings, fund raiser events, that kind of thing. She covers the shoot outs on her own time as a freelancer," Adam said.

Dustin shook his head, his protective instincts on full alert. When he could, he'd have a talk with her. Why the hell was she throwing herself into the line of fire? Covering a story wasn't worth getting killed.

Houston's eyes narrowed. "You still got a thing for her?"

"What?" Dustin feigned disinterest. "I barely know her. It's been ten years."

"Good." His younger brother's lips curled in a devious grin. "Then I guess you won't mind if I ask her out while I'm in town?"

"Don't push it," Dustin warned. "I said I barely know her. I might pay her a visit though, while I'm here." What would it hurt? And maybe he could talk some sense into her crazy head.

"Pay who a visit?" Their mother strode through the door and headed for the coffee maker.

"No one," Dustin answered.

31

"His old girlfriend from high school."

His mother poured cup of coffee and turned to face Dustin. "Jenna Turner?"

Dustin frowned. "Yeah. You remember her?"

"I'm your mother. How could I forget how broken-hearted you were when she dumped you?"

"I wasn't brokenhearted," Dustin insisted. "And she didn't dump me. We parted ways in mutual agreement. She wanted an adventurous life, and so did I. We knew we wouldn't get that as a married couple."

"Oh, I don't know. Your father and I have had our share of adventures."

His lips curling on the corners, Dustin said, "Face it, Mom, your sense of adventure is taking a different route home from the grocery store."

She raised her steaming paper cup of coffee to her lips and sipped carefully, grimacing. "You don't know how much adventure we had before you boys were born. Why I can tell you stories about our cross-country trip across the U.S. with nothing but a couple of backpacks, the clothes on our backs and our love." His mother's gaze softened and shifted toward the door. "I hope he's doing okay."

Dustin refocused his attention on his family. When his father made it through surgery—and he would, the man was too stubborn to kick it this soon—Dustin would knock on Jenna's door and tell her what he thought of her chasing crime and nearly being killed.

The news producer at the station had been

impressed with Jenna and Toby's coverage of the hostage crisis and promised to look at anything she came up with in the future. Unfortunately, tornadoes sweeping across the southeast trumped her local hostage crisis, and the report never made it to national news.

If all went well with Dustin's father, Jenna would execute Operation Get-Dustin-Out-Of-My-System. She planned on luring the SEAL to her apartment for the night and making sweet love into the wee hours of the morning. That should be enough to give her a taste of the new and improved Dustin Ford. It would also prove to her that her teenage infatuation with the man was only that...an infatuation of an immature mind. In the morning, he'd go his way, she'd go hers, and she'd be over him for good.

A shiver slipped down her spine at the thought of Dustin in her apartment...hot and naked, lying in her bed, or on her living room rug, or standing in her kitchen, ready to take her on the dining table. She practically felt the cool wood beneath her bare bottom, and another shiver slipped across her skin.

Her body heated, and she switched the thermostat lower. On her way to the store, she'd gotten Adam Ford's number from her cousin at the police station, and from Adam she'd gotten Dustin's number, claiming she had something he dropped earlier in the lobby of the hospital. Adam told her he would pass on the message, but she insisted she wanted to speak with Dustin herself. She'd asked about their father, who'd still been in surgery at the time she called.

"I'll keep him and your family in my thoughts and prayers." Damn, his father must be in bad shape to be in surgery that long. Instead of heading back to her apartment, she returned to the hospital and parked in the huge lot, tucking the little pink bag of naughty undergarments between the seats in case Dustin rode home with her.

Inside the medical facility, she learned Mr. Ford had been moved to Cardiac ICU. That was good news. He was in recovery.

Jenna let go of the breath she'd been holding and took the elevator to the correct floor. When she emerged, she headed for the waiting room, sure that not all of the Fords would be allowed to enter the CICU so soon after surgery. She'd find one of them there.

Three men looked up when she entered. All three had dark hair and brown eyes and were tall, ripped with muscles and could easily intimidate the weak with their fierce warrior-like personas.

Not Jenna. She'd known them as teenagers, growing up wild on a ranch outside of town. Granted, they were much more filled out and powerful-looking now. But only one stirred her blood. The one in the middle. Dustin.

He stepped forward, holding out his hand. "Jenna, what are you doing here?"

Jenna took his hand in hers. "I was worried about your father and wanted to come lend my moral support to his speedy recovery." For a brief moment, she glanced up into Dustin's eyes and fell into their dark depths. The intensity of his gaze burned through her and made her afraid that this experiment to get him out of her system might just backfire. As quickly as their gazes connected, she looked around him to his brothers.

Dustin tugged her closer and slipped his arm around her waist. "Jenna, you remember my brothers, Adam and Houston."

Warmth stole over her and she fought to keep from leaning into Dustin's hard body. She focused on the brothers as, one by one, she shook hands with them. Then she asked of all three, "How is he?"

"The doctor said he made it through surgery just fine," Adam said. "The next twenty-four hours will be critical."

"The CICU nurses will keep a close watch on him," Houston said. "They'll take good care of Dad."

Adam nodded. "Mom's going to stay the night here at the hospital in the waiting room."

"What about the rest of you? Are you staying in town or going back out to the ranch?" Jenna asked, her heart fluttering, as she braced herself for their response.

"I'm heading back to the ranch," Adam said. "Mom asked me to collect a few things for her, and I want to check on the foreman and see if he needs help with the animals."

"I'll probably ride with Adam." Houston rubbed hand over his chin. "I could use a shower and a shave. Then I'm coming back here to be with Mom for the night. But there's no use in all of us sleeping in the waiting room."

Which left Dustin.

She cleared her throat and smiled at Houston. "I have an apartment not far from here, with a spare bedroom if you need a place to stay close to the hospital." Heat rose in her cheeks and she willed it away. "You don't need to spend money on a hotel if you want to stay closer to your mother and father."

"Thanks," Houston said. "I really need to go to the ranch. I didn't bring much with me. I'm hoping to borrow some clothes from Adam or Dad as well as a razor and shaving cream. And when I'm not hanging out with Mom here at the hospital, I'll stay at the ranch."

Her heart thumping hard against her ribs, Jenna turned to Dustin. "What about you?"

He hadn't said a word since she she'd offered to let them stay at her apartment. His gaze bored into hers with the power to make her entire body burn. "I've been awake over forty-eight hours. I could use a real bed, but I'd like to be closer to the hospital in case Mom needs me in a hurry."

Butterflies erupted in Jenna's belly and heat rose into her cheeks.

Houston commented. "There's a hotel across from the hospital."

"I'm a couple blocks away. You could be here almost as fast," she said, her voice wavering, her courage shrinking under Dustin's enigmatic look. When he didn't answer immediately, she chickened out. "Look, the offer stands for any of you. You need a place to stay in town. You're welcome to come stay with me." She pulled a card out of her purse, jotted her address on the back and handed it to Adam since Dustin wasn't responding.

At that moment, her cell phone vibrated in her purse. She grabbed it like a lifeline to keep her from looking again into Dustin's eyes. A text message flashed across the screen from a number she didn't recognize.

I need your help. Can you meet me at the farmer's market at closing time? Rebecca

Her stomach clenched and her attention shifted from the men in the room to her own family issues. She dug her spare key out of her wallet and handed it to Adam as well. "That key will get you in."

With a quick glance Dustin's way, she hurried out of the room, embarrassment making her feet move faster.

Had she misread his interest from when he'd plowed into her earlier? When she'd broken off their engagement ten years ago, she'd been pretty harsh, knowing the only way to get him to follow his dreams was to cut his ties with her and their hometown. Had she been too effective?

Convinced he was completely over her, Jenna jabbed at the down button on the elevator, her vision blurring through a rush of tears. She missed, blinked and tried again.

A hand descended on her arm and turned her around.

She knew without looking up that Dustin stood in front of her.

"Why?"

Jenna swallowed hard in an attempt to force down the lump lodged in her throat. "Why what?" she whispered.

"Why did you offer your apartment?"

She shrugged refusing to look up. "I know how hard it is when your family is in the hospital. Staying in a hotel is so...impersonal. I would have offered a place to stay for any of my friends."

"Yeah, but we're not friends," he said, his voice tightening.

She lifted a shoulder and let it fall, her chest so tight she could barely draw a breath. "Yeah, but I had hoped you would have forgiven me by now." Her voice faded off.

Dustin's fingers dug into her arm, and he lifted her chin with his other hand. "You were pretty clear ten years ago that you didn't want anything to do with me. Have you changed your mind?"

She shook her head. "No." And it was true. She hadn't changed her mind, because she'd never stopped loving this man. Hell, this experiment was going to blow up in her face and reopen all the emotion she'd felt at the time she'd pushed him away so many years ago. "Forget it. I thought you and your brothers could use a little help. If it's uncomfortable for you because of our past relationship, no worries. You can put the key in the mail. Now, I have to go." Her eyes filled with tears, and she jerked away from him.

The bell dinged, the elevator door slid open and Jenna rushed in, turning slowly, hoping the doors would close before Dustin saw the tears in her eyes.

He stared straight into her eyes, his brow puckering slightly. "Thanks for stopping by to check on Dad."

The doors slid closed and Jenna could swear she heard Dustin whisper something that sounded like I missed you.

She shook her head, sure she was projecting her own thoughts on him. So much for buying new panties. The man clearly wasn't interested, or hadn't forgiven her for being so brutal in brushing off their engagement. And she sure as hell wasn't going to tell him that she'd sacrificed her own happiness so that he could follow his dream. How pathetic would that look after all these years?

Jenna hurried to her SUV, brushing the tears from her cheeks. She called Toby and choked out the message she'd received from Rebecca. "God, I hope we're not headed into another disaster. Waco doesn't need more lunatics like David Koresh and the Branch Davidians in '93. But who knows what's happening behind their walls? I'm going to check it out. Be ready with your camera in case there's trouble at the commune."

4

Dustin walked back into the waiting room where his brothers stood, arms crossed over their chests, eyebrows elevated.

"Well?" Adam asked.

Dustin frowned. "Well what?"

"Are you going to stay at her apartment, or not?" Houston prompted.

"It's really none of your business."

Adam held up the key, his lips twisting as if he was working hard at not smiling. "Then I guess you won't be needing this."

Dustin held out his hand. "Give it to me, and I'll be sure it gets back to her."

His older brother snatched the key out of his reach. "Uh-uh. She ditched you ten years ago. Houston and I discussed it. We're not letting you get sucked into her web again. She's bad news."

Houston chuckled. "News, get it?"

With a scowl, Dustin wiggled his fingers. "Give me the damned key. I don't care what she is. I'm not a teenager anymore. What happened in the past was for the best. If we'd gotten married, I wouldn't be a SEAL."

"How do you know that?" Houston asked. "You always wanted to be a SEAL. You could have done it—even married."

Dustin shook his head. "If Jenna and I had married, I wouldn't have enlisted. I would have done like Adam and gone on to college. Probably would have had a decent desk job where I wouldn't be shot at."

"Huh. I went to college, but now I'm getting shot at," Adam pointed out. "You would have shriveled up and died behind a desk. The three of us never did like being indoors."

Adam was right. From the time they learned to walk, they'd been outside every minute of daylight and sometimes well past dark, if their mother didn't put her foot down. "Whatever. I'm old enough and more experienced. I can manage a night at Jenna's apartment without falling apart. It's just a place to stay."

Adam crossed his arms. "So is the hotel across the street."

"I'd rather not spend the money when I have Jenna's apartment available."

"And you're not going there to get laid?" Houston shook his head even before Dustin could respond. "Don't even try to lie. She's hot. You had a thing for her. Old flames don't always die. They come back and scorch us, if we let them."

"Says a man who's never had a serious girlfriend." Dustin waved a hand at his younger brother. "When was the last time you got laid?"

Houston squirmed. "Last week."

Dustin's eyebrows shot up. "You were in training. Unless you got a thing for guys, it's been longer than that. Try again."

"Okay, it's been more than a month."

"Who was she? What was her name?"

"I don't know. I met her at a bar."

"Exactly. You haven't had a real relationship. Ever. So how do you know if an old flame will scorch me or not?"

"Who has time for more than a quick hop in the sack? I give one hundred and ten percent to the force." Houston tipped his head at Dustin. "Same as you. I haven't heard about you having a steady girl."

"Same issue as you. My job takes everything." He held out his hand to Adam. "Give me the damned key."

Adam laid the key in Dustin's hand. "We just don't want to see you get hurt."

"You two are so kind." Dustin's tone dripped sarcasm. "I'm a big boy. I can handle it." He pocketed the key, the metal burning against his thigh. "Besides, I'm curious what she wants out of this."

"She's probably kicking herself for dumping you and is going to beg you to take her back."

"I doubt it." But if she did beg him to take her back,

he'd have the pleasure of blowing her off this time. Hell, he hadn't been with a woman in over six months, having been too busy to even care. If Jenna wanted to invite him into her bed, who was he to disappoint the woman? He could have sex with her and easily walk away. Just like she'd done to him.

He scrubbed a hand over his face, tired beyond belief.

"You look like hell." Adam clapped a hand on his back. "Why don't you head to Jenna's apartment now and get some sleep?"

"I want to see Dad first."

"Yeah. Me, too," Houston said. "Then it's home to sleep for twenty-four hours."

After spending some time sitting with his father while his mother and siblings went to eat dinner, Dustin was more than ready to reset his internal clock. His body didn't know if it was day or night, and jet lag was dragging his eyelids closed even when he stood. He stretched out in the chair next to his father's bed, his legs crossed at the ankles.

Seeing his father fresh from surgery had been a blow. The man was pale beneath his rancher's tan. With tubes poking out of his arms and nose, and wires connected to electrodes on his chest, he looked like something from a science-fiction movie, not the robust man Dustin knew and loved.

His parents were getting older. They wouldn't be around forever.

Was now the time to make the break from the service and come home?

Dustin fingered the key in his pocket. Was now the time to rekindle an old flame and see if there was still fuel to feed the fire? Or had Jenna's offer been nothing more than an old friend extending a helping hand in a time of need?

There was only one way to find out.

His mother entered the room. "Dustin, you must be exhausted. Go home."

He sighed and stretched. "Where are Adam and Houston?"

"Gone to the ranch to help take care of things. Your father probably won't wake until morning. Get some sleep, or you'll scare him with your haggard face."

"Thanks, Mom. Nothing like laying it out there without sugar-coating." Dustin stood, stretched and hugged his mother. "Everything seems to be working as it should. His heartbeat is steady and he seems to be sleeping comfortably. Are you sure you don't want me to stay the night with him?"

She shook her head. "No. I want to be here in case he wakes. He's likely to be cranky, and I want to spare the nurses his temper."

Dustin chuckled. "He never was a good patient."

"No, but he'll listen to me when I tell him he's being an ass."

"You do have a knack for getting through to him. Call me if you need anything. I'll be in town, not far away."

She cupped his cheek. "I hope you know what you're getting into, Dustin."

"Adam and Houston told you where I'm staying?"

She nodded.

"I'll be fine. I'm all grown up now."

"Yes, but you loved her enough to ask her to marry you. Beware your heart doesn't get broken again."

"Thank, Mom, but I can handle it. It's only a place to stay. Like a hotel room, only free." Hugging his mother one last time, Dustin left the room.

Jenna sped through the streets of Waco, her foot hard on the accelerator before she realized just how fast she was going.

Damn. With Dustin back in town, you'd think her mind had clouded. She couldn't put together two coherent thoughts. He was just a man...a very sexy... incredibly muscled man... but still, only a man.

She refused to let herself get all wrapped up in him again. She wasn't a naive teen anymore. The man had stayed away for the past ten years, apparently only coming to Waco to visit his parents and then heading right back to his duty assignment. If he'd had any lingering feelings for her, he'd have looked her up, maybe asked if she wanted to go out.

Then again, she'd been pretty blunt, telling him she wasn't interested in settling down, that being married to him would cramp her style and force her to give up too many of her own goals and dreams.

In truth, she had given up her main dream of being a

permanent part of Dustin's life so that he could pursue his lifelong dream of being a Navy SEAL. She sucked in a long, deep breath and let it out slowly to regulate the erratic beat of her heart.

She had to focus on her cousin's message and get to her before the farmer's market closed.

Rebecca was a cousin on her mother's side. Rebecca's mother, Jenna's Aunt Lissa, was a free spirit, who left her first husband to live with a bearded man in a run-down cabin near the river. She was sort of like a cross between a hippie and a puritan, sewing her own clothes, growing her vegetables and making handcrafted items she sold or bartered for other things she might need.

Rebecca's father had taken Aunt Lissa to court for custody of his daughter Rebecca and won. He remarried and raised her like most normal children with access to electronics, television and movies. But her relationship with her father's new wife wasn't good, and she often retreated into her bedroom whenever she was at home, escaping into video games. Her behavior had become more and more belligerent toward her stepmother until her father punished her by taking away all of her electronics.

Angry, she'd thrown a screaming fit.

Jenna's mother had stepped in, offering to take Rebecca for the rest of the school semester and to watch out for her during the summer. At his wit's end, her father had agreed.

Rebecca's rebellion seemed to calm until one day she

disappeared, leaving behind a note that she'd gone to live with her mother in the Sweet Salvation commune outside of Waco, claiming she wanted a simpler life, free of advanced technology and peer pressure. This from a girl who'd been addicted to online gaming.

On the one hand, she'd kicked her gaming addiction —on the other, she'd fallen in with the zealot teachings of the commune's elders. She'd convinced her father she was happier and living a good life. Her father, trying to hold together his marriage, reluctantly agreed to let her stay at the commune.

Rebecca had been there for over a year now, turned seventeen and seemed to be assimilating to the lifestyle. Thus Jenna's surprise when she received a text message from a member of a community that shunned cell phone usage, computers, televisions and electricity that wasn't produced by their myriad of windmills scattered around a six-hundred acre compound.

Jenna hurried to the farmer's market, afraid it would close before she arrived, and she'd miss Rebecca. The members of the commune were brought to the market in trucks with their fresh vegetables and handmade crafts to sell. All proceeds were returned to the commune to be distributed equally. When the market closed, they were loaded into the trucks and returned to the Sweet Salvation compound where the women had their chores and the men had theirs.

Jenna frequented the market during the cooler days of late fall, avoiding the scorching hot days like the day was turning out to be. It wasn't a fire or a gas line exploding, but at least her cousin's call for help kept her from mooning over the tragedy that was her love life. From the message Rebecca had sent, the girl probably wasn't happy with the way things were going and wanted out.

Parking near the market, Jenna jumped out and hurried toward the simple booth, craftily constructed for ease of erecting and tearing down in a hurry. Several women dressed in old-fashioned gingham dresses stood behind the counter, offering samples of homemade jellies. Rebecca was nowhere to be seen.

In an attempt not to appear too obvious, Jenna wandered past the booth to the next one where aprons and bonnets were sold. Again, no Rebecca. Afraid she was too late, Jenna kept walking to the end of the row of vendors, circled around behind the booths and stepped over extension cords and empty boxes.

"Jenna!" A voice called out from the direction of the portable toilets.

Rebecca's head poked out of the door of the one on the far end, and she waved Jenna toward her.

When Jenna reached the portable bathroom, Rebecca's hand snaked out and dragged her into the molded plastic room.

The smell of human waste struck Jenna, and she forced back her gag reflex, worried about her cousin who'd gone to great lengths to get her there.

"I don't have much time." Rebecca whispered.

"What's wrong?" Jenna gripped the girl's arms. "Are you being treated badly? Anyone abusing you?"

Rebecca had lost her baby-fat from the last time Jenna had seen her. With her strawberry-blond hair pulled back into a tight bun and her pale, freckled face glowing with a layer of perspiration, completely devoid of makeup, she appeared older. She wore a light green gingham dress and serviceable white shoes, the kind Jenna's grandmother wore before she'd passed away. "They want me to marry one of the elders when I turn eighteen next month." Her cousin's chin lowered. "I try to be a good follower, but I can't do it." She looked up, her eyes filled with tears. "I just can't."

"You don't have to marry anyone you don't want to. You can move back in with your father."

Before Jenna finished her sentence, Rebecca was shaking her head. "I can't. My stepmother hates me."

"You can move in with me."

"The courts won't let that happen. Nor would my father. I have to stick it out at least until I turn eighteen, but then I want out."

"Are you sure you're safe?"

"No one has harmed me yet. And the life there is pretty decent, for the most part."

"What do you mean, 'the most part'?"

She shrugged. "It all seems on the up and up. People like hard work and making things with their hands, using their brains and natural tools to cultivate crops. On the surface they all seem happy."

Jenna tried not to breathe too deeply. The fumes were overwhelming her. "I feel there's a 'but' in there."

"I can't put my finger on it, but something's not right. Ever since the Department for Family and Protective Services visited the compound last month, the elders are spending more time in secret meetings and they seem somehow more intense. I don't think they liked being told what to do. Elder John Powell is on a preaching tear, his sermons lasting upwards of four hours, seven days a week. We can hardly get our work done. More and more of the sermons speak to the rapture and the end of the world. It's creeping me out."

Jenna hugged the girl. "You should come with me. It sounds like it's not safe there."

"I can't. My mother's still there. I can't leave the community without her." Rebecca bit her bottom lip and stared down at her hands, bunched in the muted gingham fabric of her dress. "A couple other things. And I'm not sure whether they mean anything, but there are late-night deliveries to the main building. I snuck out of our dorm one night and found men unloading wooden crates, carrying them into the worship hall. I don't know what was in them, but I don't think it was food or staples. When I entered the hall the next day, there was no sign of the crates. I think they stored them in the basement—which they keep locked."

"The boxes could contain food, clothing, or farming supplies. Why are you worried?"

"I wouldn't have mentioned them, except the deliveries started coming soon after an outsider joined the community who doesn't seem to fit in. He reminds me of some of the guys on my old combat video games. You know...the kind that kick butt and don't put up with much. Not at all like most of the men in the community." Her brows pinched. "Well except Elder Snow." She looked up at Jenna. "It could be nothing, but in case it's something, I thought I'd mention it"

"Do you want me to come out and bring you and your mother out of there? Will she come?"

Rebecca's eyes widened. "You can't. They won't let you past the gates. You have to go through their orientation and sign a contract before you're allowed inside the compound. And then you're not allowed to talk about what goes on inside." Rebecca touched Jenna's arm. "You can't take this public. You can't make it one of your news reports. They'll know it was me." Her eyes grew rounder. "Please tell me you won't do a story on this. Please."

Jenna wanted to blow the entire compound wide open, exposing the elders for the bastard zealots they were, frightening women and children into doing their bidding, marrying men they didn't love. Who knew what else was going on behind the walls of the compound? "I promise not to shoot a story about this. But I can't just stand back and do nothing."

Rebecca held up a disposable cell phone. "I bought this with money I stole from the commune. I know it was wrong, but I wanted to be able to let someone who cared know what was happening in case things go wrong. I could be imagining it, but I have a bad feeling."

"How are you able to hide the phone?"

"I stuff it into my undergarments and turned off the sound and vibration."

"What happens if they find it?"

Rebecca ducked her head. "At best, they'll confiscate it."

"At worst?"

She shrugged and looked away. "I've seen them publicly whip people who break the rules."

Jenna's fists tightened. "Children, too?"

She shook her head. "Maybe not the little ones, but definitely kids my age."

"Oh, honey." Jenna pulled Rebecca into her arms. "Let me take you home with me. Don't go back. We'll figure out some way to get your mother out of there."

Rebecca hugged her tight, sniffling. "I can't leave her, and she's so brainwashed, she'll do anything they tell her to."

"You've been there a year, so why are you not marching to their tune?"

The color in her cheeks darkened. "I met a boy I like. I don't want to marry the elder."

So Rebecca had a reason other than her mother holding her at the compound.

"Does he want to leave, too?" Jenna asked.

Her cheeks bloomed with color. "He sounded like he'd be willing to go, if I go."

"I'll see what I can do."

"Just don't take it to the news. Because we're related, they'll know it was me."

"I'll keep it on the down low," Jenna assured her, not certain what she could do to help the girl. "Now, you better get back. I think the women were packing up their goods. Go first. I'll wait a minute or two and leave after that."

"Thanks, Jenna. I didn't know who else to call."

"Hang onto that phone, sweetie. Use it if you have to."

"I will." She lifted her dress and apron and tucked the phone into the waistband of her underwear. When she smoothed the dress down over her hips and straightened her apron, the bulge of the phone was impossible to discern. Rebecca peeked out of the portable potty, dragged in a breath and stepped out, closing the door behind her.

Jenna gave her a full two minutes before she ventured out.

A woman in a gingham dress stood nearby, as if waiting her turn to use the facilities.

With a friendly smile, Jenna stepped past her and turned away from the booths where the Sweet Salvation women were almost finished dismantling the wooden counter and shelves. Out of the corner of her eye, Jenna picked out Rebecca, her head down, working quietly alongside the other women. An older female glanced up, her gaze following Jenna as she stopped at a booth selling eggplants.

Jenna fished a five out of her purse and paid for two of the dark purple vegetables. The farmer offered to wrap them in a recycled plastic bag, but Jenna thanked him and slid them into her large purse.

By the time she'd completed her purchase, the group from Sweet Salvation had loaded their belongings into the old pickup trucks, and Rebecca was seated in the front of one between two older women. She didn't glance toward Jenna, and Jenna didn't expect her to. The whole situation reeked of creepy. Somehow, she had to get inside that compound and find out what was going on. In the meantime, she needed to get to the station and see if she had any assignments from her boss.

She sighed, wondering what social event was taking place that day or what new business was cutting its ribbon in the Waco area. She enjoyed working as a reporter, meeting new people and sharing local events, but sometimes, it seemed so meaningless when there were real issues and problems out there that should be on the news.

After covering a world trade organization afternoon meeting with the trade minister from the Netherlands and a new brewery ribbon-cutting ceremony in downtown Waco, the sun was on its way down, and she still hadn't heard anything from Dustin, which was just as well. She didn't have time to waste on a relationship doomed to failure. Dustin was a Navy SEAL stationed out of Virginia. Jenna was a small city news reporter, her roots firmly planted in her hometown.

Dustin was following his dream and she was following hers. Their lives were pretty much mutually exclusive. She shoved her hair off her forehead, glad the brutal sun was setting. It had been in the hundreds every afternoon for the past week, and it wasn't getting any cooler. If they didn't get rain soon, the lakes and rivers would dry up. Already the city water department had instituted water rationing to conserve what little they had in the aquifers and reservoirs.

Jenna stepped out of her SUV, climbed the steps to her apartment and let herself in, not really looking forward to a lonely night eating leftover pizza. She remembered the eggplants in her purse and snorted. She didn't have ingredients to make stuffed eggplant. Tomorrow, she'd invite Toby over and cook for him. The two of them ate entirely too many meals from fast-food restaurants on the run between news events.

Setting her purse on the counter in the kitchen, Jenna cocked her head at the sound of running water. She turned toward the wall connecting her apartment to the next. But no, the water sound was coming from the other side of her bedroom door, which was closed.

The only time she closed her bedroom door was when her mother dropped by unexpectedly and she hadn't made her bed.

Her pulse quickened, and she edged toward her bedroom. Her first thought was that an intruder had entered her home. She quickly nixed that conclusion. What intruder would take the time to shower?

The next thought sent butterflies fluttering through her belly. Had one of the Ford men taken her up on her offer to stay the night? If so, which one?

Please let it be Dustin.

Her heart lodged firmly in her throat, Jenna twisted the doorknob and entered the darkened bedroom. A light shined beneath the door of the bathroom. The water shut off.

Sucking her bottom lip between her teeth, Jenna closed the distance between her and the bathroom door, raising her hand to knock. She hesitated. What if it wasn't Dustin? What if Adam or Houston had accepted her offer? They were equally handsome men, but neither of the two were the one Jenna hadn't forgotten over the past ten years.

With her hand poised to knock, she froze. Maybe she shouldn't appear too eager. Men didn't like to be chased. They liked to do the chasing. Before she could turn and run back into the living room, the door opened and Dustin's broad shoulders filled the gap.

The air seized in Jenna's lungs, and she stood with her hand still raised, her fist clenched to rap on the door.

Dustin's lips quirked upward on the corners. "I hope you don't mind. I waited for an hour, but couldn't stand it any longer. I hadn't had a shower since I left Virginia and, since there wasn't soap or shampoo in the guest shower, I used yours."

Her gaze drifted downward over his bare chest and lower still to the towel he had loosely wrapped, riding low on his hips. One yank and it would fall, exposing him.

Jenna clenched her fingers tightly to keep from reaching out. Hell, she wasn't a girl playing silly games with a boy. She was a grown woman with raging physical needs, and Dustin was just the man to satisfy her every desire.

He'd been pretty amazing as a teen, making love to her as though he worshiped her. Everywhere he'd touched her with his fingers or lips had sizzled. Her memories were so clear, she could almost feel the warmth of his hand sliding down her back, cupping her naked ass and lifting her onto the tailgate of his pickup as he stepped between her legs and made sweet love to her.

Focus, Turner, she reminded herself. Just because Dustin wore only a towel around his waist, didn't mean he was coming on to her. He'd taken a shower because he wanted to feel clean after traveling halfway around the world.

As her gaze rested on the towel around his waist, it tented.

Holy hell, he wasn't immune to her after all.

5

Standing naked in front of a beautiful woman would have made any man hard—especially if that woman was staring with as much longing in her eyes as Jenna was. His jaw clenched and he fought for control, but his cock had a will of its own and it was getting harder by the second.

"If you'll excuse me, I'll get dressed," he started to step around her, but she didn't move. Short of pushing her out of the way, he couldn't reach the clean clothing he'd left in his duffle bag. Which meant he was stuck in a tenting towel that barely covered his hips and would soon expose a whole lot more as he jutted out under her fixed stare.

Fine. If she wasn't moving, he'd move her himself. He released the corners of the towel and let it drop to the floor, then gripped Jenna's arms, lifted her firmly and set her to the side. "Thank you." His shoulders back, head held high and back ramrod straight, he strode naked through her bedroom to the living room where he'd left his bag.

If he wasn't mistaken, that tiny whoosh of air behind him was her gasp. Of surprise, anger or desire, he wasn't sure, but he'd sure as hell given her something to think about by strutting through her home in nothing but his birthday suit.

Grabbing a pair of running shorts, he stepped into them and pulled them up around his hips before he turned to face her.

She stood in the doorway to her bedroom, having followed him out to the living room. Twin pink flags flew high in her cheeks. Slowly, she leaned against the doorjamb, her lips curving into a smile that was a little too strained to be natural.

"Glad you made yourself at home. Don't feel like you have to dress on my account. It's not as if I haven't seen you naked before."

"If it's all the same to you, it's been a long time." Her blatant stare made his cock even harder. Perhaps he'd have been better off in a pair of jeans that would smash his jutting erection against his belly instead of allowing it to poke out at an embarrassing angle.

Her lips twitched and she stared for a moment longer before she straightened. "I'm going to get a shower." Jenna turned away and slid her jacket off her shoulders, revealing a spaghetti strap camisole beneath.

The pencil skirt and camisole did almost as much to him as if she'd been standing there naked. Her clothing emphasized her curves and made him long to strip her of them, one piece at time.

"If you want to order pizza, the number is on the fridge," she called out over her shoulder, her fingers on the zipper at her side. She dragged the tab down and shimmied out of the skirt, letting it fall to the floor. Standing in the black camisole and minuscule underwear, she faced him, still wearing the silver stilettos. "I like pepperoni on my pizza."

He stood staring as, once again, she turned away, dragged the camisole over her head and tossed it onto the bed. The black, lace panties and a matching bra with silver stilettos should have been outlawed on her body.

Dustin swallowed hard on the groan rising up his throat. As casually as he could, he answered, "Pepperoni it is." Dustin cursed the way his voice caught, tight in his throat. He coughed and said. "I'll order."

As Jenna neared the bathroom door, she reached behind her and unclipped her bra. "Thanks." She tossed the garment onto the bed and entered the bathroom, turning to close the door, offering him a view of her full, rounded breasts.

Sweet heaven. Dustin spun and raked his hand through his hair, wishing he'd had time to get it cut. Ah hell, it didn't matter. If he had a lick of sense, he'd leave. Now. Before Jenna came out of the shower, smelling like honeysuckle shampoo. He'd be putty in her hands, willing to do anything she wanted as long as it included getting naked with her and making love until dawn.

All vestiges of exhaustion flew out the window as his blood raced through his veins and downward to fill his hardening shaft.

If he'd had any doubts about the reason she'd invited him to her apartment, she'd erased them in the flick of her zipper sliding down her hip.

Dustin paced the length of the tiny living room, forcing himself to think, to breathe, and get his shit together. For the first time in ten years, he felt like that kid he'd been when he'd given his virginity to the girl he'd thought was his one and only true love, sweet Jenna Turner. His childish brain had been convinced she'd felt the same, harbored the same depth of love and devotion for him as he had for her.

That's right, remember who did the dumping.

If she wanted to get it on again, then okay. He didn't have to confuse desire with love this time. Neither had to be tied down with the crippling effects of love and the co-dependency of the emotion. Especially when one of them wasn't that into the other.

The water switched on in the bathroom, setting Dustin's imagination on fire with images of Jenna standing naked beneath the spray, water running through her glorious hair, down her back and sweeping off the curve of her ass. She'd turn and let the water run down her front, dripping off the tips of her rosy nipples.

Dustin would lean forward and lick the moisture off her breasts and suck one into his mouth, pulling just hard enough.

Jenna would wrap her arms around the back of his head and drag him closer, like she had when they'd made love in their favorite swimming hole, that magical place where a sharp bend in the creek made a natural pool.

The water switched off, and Dustin remembered he was supposed to call in an order for pizza. He dragged his gaze away from the bathroom door and dove for his cell phone. In less than three minutes he placed the order for a large pepperoni pizza. When he hung up, he shot a glance through her bedroom to the bathroom door.

At that moment, Jenna emerged, wearing a wrap of sheer black fabric that did little to hide her curves. Her gaze captured his, and her eyelids lowered.

Damn. Hunger burned through his veins that had nothing to do with cheesy pepperoni pizza and everything to do with the woman flaunting her perfect body.

Sucking in an unsteady breath, Dustin strode forward, determined to get to the bottom of her game. "Jenna." He came to a stop in front of her, his breathing ragged as if he'd been running through a swamp in full gear.

"Yes, Dustin?" she gazed up at him through her eyelashes, raised her hand to sweep the wet hair back behind her ear. Her wrap drifted open, revealing a perky breast and the shadowy tuft of hair cloaking her sex.

He gripped her arms, the electricity that shot through him scrambling his brain cells. Instead of shaking her and holding her at arm's length, he gathered her close and buried his face in the long column of her neck. "What are you doing?"

"What do you want me to do?" she asked, her voice breathy, her fingers curling around the back of his neck, urging him closer.

"I want you to stay out of my life."

"Really?" She leaned her head to the side, giving him better access to the pulse beating at the base of her throat. "You have a funny way of showing it." Her hands slipped over his shoulders and down his arms, finding their way around his waist. "If you wanted me to leave you alone, you wouldn't have come here tonight."

God, he hated when she was right. He didn't want to leave her alone, nor did he want her to leave him alone. From the moment he'd fallen over her in the hospital, he'd imagined holding her in his arms, brushing his lips across her naked skin, making sweet love to her through the night.

Dustin pulled away from that frantically fluttering pulse and leaned his cheek against her temple. "Why now?"

"I guess you could say I wanted to see if what we'd felt for each other when we were teens was still there."

He didn't say anything, afraid that if he did, he'd admit that old flame was blazing, every time he touched her. Hell, he didn't even have to touch her to get excited by her. But that didn't mean anything. At least not to her. "As I recall, you gave me the heave-ho. You were very clearly done with me back then."

She lifted her shoulders and let them fall. "Would you have stayed had we married?"

His fingers tightened on her arms. "Hell, yes."

She smiled up at him and cupped his chin. "Maybe I wasn't ready to be tied down." Jenna leaned up on her toes. "We were young, and thought we knew everything." Her lips brushed across his.

He wanted to ignore how soft they were, to hang on tight to his anger at being dumped, but he couldn't. Not when she was warm and willing in his arms.

Dustin dragged her body against his. "If we do this tonight, it doesn't change anything."

She blinked and then nodded. "Okay."

"Don't expect that we'll pick up where we left off."

"I won't." She pressed her fingers into the back of his neck, angling his head downward as she rose on her toes, her lips hovering close to his. "Now, are you going to kiss me, or do I have to beg?"

The thought of her begging made his cock rock hard, and he couldn't think past the way her breasts pressed against his naked chest.

Dustin bent, grabbed the backs of her thighs and lifted her.

Gripping his shoulders, Jenna wrapped her legs around his waist and lowered herself until his shaft nudged her entrance, through the fabric of his shorts.

Dustin grimaced and then lifted her swiftly up and away, though his instinct was to drive into her hard and fast. "Protection," he gritted out.

"In my nightstand." She tightened her legs around him and leaned forward, her breasts bobbing in his face.

Dustin captured a nipple between his teeth through the sheer garment and tapped it with the tip of his tongue.

Jenna's back arched. She reached between them and shifted the robe to the side so that he had unencumbered access, and he latched on, pulling hard.

"Hey! Nibble, don't bite." Though her words were warning, she urged his mouth across her chest, giving him the other nipple to chew on.

A man could only hold out so long before he had to be inside a women. Dustin strode toward her bedroom and laid her out on the comforter, shucked his shorts and then crawled between her legs.

"In the top drawer," she gasped. "Hurry."

He shook his head. "Uh-uh."

"What?" She stared up at him as if he'd lost his mind. "I need you. In me. Now."

"Not until you're right where I want you." He cupped her sex with his hand and slid a finger inside her. "You're not nearly ready."

She planted her heels in the mattress and lifted her hips, angling to force that finger deeper. He pulled out and slid another in. "No, you're not ready." He bent over her and claimed her lips in a long, slow kiss, then dragged his mouth across hers, his tongue lashing out, skimming the seam until she opened to him.

He thrust inside her mouth and claimed her tongue

in a long slow glide, twisting around and around until neither one of them could breathe, his plan to bring her to the edge, make love to her until she screamed out his name, and then leave her wanting more.

Revenge would be hot and sweet. This time when they parted, it would be on his terms, and he would never look back.

Jenna dragged in a lungful of air, her body on fire with desire. "Please, Dustin. Take me now. I need you inside me."

"Not yet." He brushed his lips across her chin in feather-soft kisses, tonguing, nipping and kissing his way along the curve of her neck and downward to take first one, then the other nipple into his mouth, laving the tips into tight little beads.

She threaded her fingers into his hair and held him close, encouraging him to take more. His warm, wet mouth on her made her writhe. "Please," she moaned.

Dustin moved down her body, touching each of her ribs with his tongue, dipping into her belly button before blazing a path to the mound of curls over her sex.

She let her knees fall open, exposing her entrance. In a flash of sheer lust, she almost pointed and shouted, "There! That's where I want it. Come on, baby!"

But she lay still, waiting for his next move.

And, oh, was it worth the wait.

Dustin parted her folds and blew a warm stream of air over the strip of flesh nestled between.

Nerves ignited and her belly clenched.

With the tip of his finger, he tapped her clit, sending blasts of electrical currents through her like bolts of lightning in a storm-filled sky. Her body jerked, and she pressed her heels into the mattress to lift her bottom. "Please," she moaned, her voice tight, her control slipping.

His finger traced a path from the fleshy bundle of extremely excited nerves to her dripping entrance, more than ready to accommodate his steely shaft. Jenna cupped his hand and guided his fingers into her.

Dustin leaned over her mound again and spread her folds wide, then touched her there, lashing out with his tongue, flicking, licking and sucking her into his mouth.

"Oh, sweet heaven, take me now, before I come completely apart."

"Almost there," he said, his words stirring air across her heated core. He continued to flick and swirl, his fingers pumping in and out of her channel.

Just when Jenna didn't think it could get better, the tingling took over, quickly escalating into spasms of sensation, rocketing through her, sending her flying over the edge of reason into the stratosphere.

"Dustin!" she cried aloud, grabbing him by the ears and holding on as she rode wave after wave of the most intense orgasm she'd ever experienced in her life.

As she drifted back to earth, she tugged on his ears. "Now? Please tell me you'll finish what you started."

He chuckled and rose up her body like a conquering hero. Poised over her, he kissed her, his mouth tasting like her sex, making her want him even more. Dustin rose, locking his elbows as he stared down at her. "Where did you say they were?"

She jerked her head toward the table beside the bed.

Dustin reached into the nightstand, found the condoms she'd purchased earlier that day, tore one open and rolled it quickly over himself. "Ready?"

"Hell, yeah!" She raised her legs, locking them behind his back and dug her heels into his buttocks.

Dustin thrust into her, hard, fast and all the way to the hilt. For a long moment, he remained still, his thick girth filling her, stretching her channel in a filling, delicious way. Then he pulled out, ever so slowly, taking her with him. In, then out, he moved, settling into a rhythm as old as time. Slowly at first, he built momentum until he hammered into her again and again.

Jenna rode with him until she reached her second orgasm. Her breath caught and held as her body erupted in a string of explosions, each more intense than the last.

Dustin thrust one last time, powering into her, burying himself deep, his cock throbbing against her channel. For a long, exquisite moment, they were connected, no words passing between them.

Then Dustin kissed her lips and dropped down, rolling her onto her side without pulling free.

Jenna nuzzled against his hard chest, inhaling the purely male scent of the man she still loved with all her heart. She thought she could go into this and perhaps get him out of her system once and for all, hoping and praying his skill at lovemaking had diminished over time.

Instead, he'd become more expert and knew exactly what it took to bring her to the edge and catapult her to the stars.

Based on Dustin's initial promise that making love to her would change nothing, Jenna could only anticipate another end to their tempestuous relationship. When she'd been a young, naive nineteen-year-old, she'd done what she thought was best though it broke her heart. Now, as an older, wiser twenty-nine year old with her biological clock ticking loudly, she realized that not only was this effort doomed to failure, but it resurfaced all the longing she'd pushed to the back of her mind for ten years.

Dustin had been right. Nothing had changed. On her part. She wanted Dustin Ford as much now as before, maybe more. The problem was getting him to believe her.

6

_____

Dustin woke before the sun edged above the horizon the next day. His internal clock out of whack, he couldn't go back to sleep. He took the opportunity to gaze his fill of the beautiful, auburn-haired woman lying on the pillow beside him.

For a moment he could pretend they were a happily married couple, sleeping in the same bed like all was right with their worlds. He'd wake her up with the sun, kiss her and make love to her until the light filled the sky, and they were completely satiated.

Who was he kidding? He'd never get enough of making love with this woman. A lifetime wasn't nearly enough. Sadly, he'd learned his lesson at a young age that Jenna wasn't into long-term commitment. Though could spend his life loving Jenna, she might get tired of him again and boot his ass out. He wasn't certain he could leave quietly the next time. Better not to fall in love with her again.

She stirred and turned on her side, nuzzling his chest with her cheek.

God, he wanted to hold her forever and never let her go. But Jenna was an independent woman with her own idea of how she wanted to live. He couldn't hold her any more than he could hold a wild animal in captivity. She'd break free and fly away the first chance she got.

His chest tightened at the thought of leaving at the end of the week. He'd been balls-to-the-walls busy for the past ten years. As a Navy SEAL, he was on call every hour of every day, at the whim of the DEVGRU command. If a crisis came up, they were called to neutralize the threat. Most of his team had shied away from commitment until recently. The divorce rate was high among SEALs because they were gone most of the year, either fighting dangerous missions or training. What woman wanted a man who was never around to help out?

Yet Tuck, Caesar, Remy and others had found strong women who knew what they were getting into, and accepted their relationships for what they were—intense and passionate, if somewhat sporadic. They had lives of their own, some in dangerous occupations, perhaps as dangerous as that of SEALs.

Careful not to wake Jenna, Dustin slid his arm from beneath her neck and rolled out of the bed onto his feet. He'd come home to be with his family, not with his ex-fiancé. Leaving the bedroom, he pulled the door closed behind him to keep from disturbing Jenna's sleep. As the sun filtered through the blinds, he pulled on his jeans, T-shirt and shoes. He reached for his duffle bag, hesitated and left it lying where he'd dropped it the night before, removing only his toothbrush and toothpaste. In the guest bathroom, he washed his face and brushed his teeth.

Yes, he was insane to think he could stay the week with Jenna and come out of it unscathed, but he couldn't resist spending time with her, especially after proving they still connected on a physical level. The sex was great, if not better than he remembered.

As he walked out the door, he reminded himself not to get emotionally attached. Their reunion would be short-lived.

At the hospital, he found his mother pacing in the room with his father.

She went to him, wrapping her arms around him. "I'm glad you're here."

He held her for a moment, then pushed her to arm's length, glancing over her shoulder at his father. "Has he come to yet?"

She shook her head, her eyes glistening with tears. Her face was pale and shadows had taken up residence beneath her eyes. It was as if she'd aged ten years in the time he'd been gone. He hugged her again. "You want to take a break and get something to eat?"

She shook her head. "I promised him I'd be here

when he woke up." With a weak smile, she met his gaze. "Although, I could sure use a cup of coffee."

"I smelled some brewing when I passed the waiting room. Do you want me to get some for you?"

"No, I need a walk."

"Don't worry, I'll yell down the hall if he wakes up."

She patted his cheek. "It means a lot to us that you boys made it back for his surgery. Your father said he didn't want to worry you, but he was worried himself. Until he wakes up, I won't stop worrying."

"I know." He glanced at his father, connected to tubes and wires. "That man won't go down without a fight. He's too stubborn."

"That's where you boys get your drive and determination." His mother smiled. "I'll be right back."

Left alone in the room, Dustin stepped up to his father's bedside. He'd been at the bedside of some of his friends when they'd been severely wounded, and the doctors didn't give them much of a chance to pull through. He'd seen how talking to them when they were unconscious somehow helped.

"Hey, Dad. You could have asked us to come home for a visit. You didn't have to go to all this trouble to get your boys home all at once." He tucked his thumbs in his belt loops and studied the monitor with the line and spikes measuring each heartbeat. His father's blood pressure seemed normal, and his heart was beating a strong, steady rhythm. So why wasn't he awake and badgering the nurses?

"Sun's up, Dad. Houston and Adam are helping Carson feed the animals. Are you going to sleep in while others are up and about?"

His father's eyelid twitched.

Dustin leaned forward, hope blooming in his chest. "You can hear me, can't you?"

Both eyes twitched this time.

"Have I ever told you how glad I am that you taught me how to shoot a gun?" Dustin chuckled. "Or how much I appreciate that you made us boys work hard on the ranch? I might have complained at the time, but it taught me hard work does pay off, and anything I set my mind to I can accomplish." Except when he set his mind to marrying Jenna. Everything else he'd attempted, he'd accomplished. You can't win 'em all. "Mom's worried about you. It would make her happy if you'd check in for a few minutes. Then you can go back to sleep."

His father's eyelids fluttered and opened.

A gasp behind Dustin alerted him to someone in the doorway. He turned to see his mother standing there with two cups of coffee. A smile spread across her face, making her appear ten years younger.

He turned back to his father and grinned. "Hey, Dad, I think there's someone here you'd like to see." Dustin took the coffee cups from her hands and set them on a nearby table.

"Hi, darlin'," his father lifted the hand with the IV tube taped to the back.

His mother curled her fingers around his and

squeezed gently. "About time you woke up. I thought you might sleep through the day."

"Not a chance with Dustin yammerin' about work to be done on the ranch."

"Don't you worry about the ranch," she assured him. "It'll be there when you get home."

"Makes a man want to go back to sleep." His eyelids slipped over his eyes, but a smile tugged at his dry, cracked lips.

Dustin's mother leaned over and kissed his forehead. "What are you smiling about?"

His father whispered, "I woke up."

His heart pinching hard in his chest, Dustin looked on as his mother brushed the scruffy gray hair off his father's forehead and kissed him again, tears falling from her eyes to land on his cheek.

"Hey." His father opened his eyes again. "What's with the tears? I ain't dead."

"Exactly." She kissed him again and laid her cheek against his. "And I'm truly grateful for that."

Dustin backed out of the room to give his parents some privacy and almost ran into Adam and Houston.

Adam looked over Dustin's shoulder. "What's happening?"

"Is Dad..." Houston's face blanched.

"He's fine." Dustin nodded toward the room. "Go see for yourself. He's even grumpy."

Both of his brothers expelled the air from their lungs.

"Thank God." Adam shoved a hand through his dark

hair, standing it on end. "I'll just see for myself." He entered the room to stand beside his mother, resting a hand on her shoulder.

She beamed up at him. "He woke up."

"Damn right, I woke up," his father's weak voice barely carried out into the hallway. "Feel like an old mule sat on my chest."

Houston chuckled. "And it begins."

"He'll give the nurses hell." Dustin grinned, a weight of worry lifting from his shoulders. "Say hello to Dad. He'll be happy to see you. In his own way."

Adam backed out of the room and let Houston show his face. "He looks like hell, but if he's got the energy to be grumpy, he'll be going home sooner than the doctor predicted."

"Come on, I'll buy you a cup of coffee in the waiting room." Dustin led the way to the room down the hall and poured coffee into two paper cups. He handed one to Adam.

Houston wasn't far behind. "He's going back to sleep. Mom opted to stay with him."

Dustin handed him the other cup and poured a third.

"So what's next?" Houston asked.

"We make sure Mom gets some rest and help out until we have to leave." Dustin sipped the hot liquid, grimacing at the bitterness.

"Carson had everything under control at the ranch," Adam reported. "Houston and I fed the animals while

Carson went out to ride the fences and make sure the bull wasn't visiting the neighbor's herd."

Houston stretched and yawned. "I slept like a baby in my old bed. It was a nice change from sleeping on the hard ground."

"Have you considered getting out of the Army?" Dustin asked his younger brother.

Houston shook his head. "Sometimes I think it would be nice to have time off occasionally, maybe even get a girlfriend."

Adam snorted, nearly spewing coffee. He set his cup down and coughed until he cleared the fluid from his throat. "You make it sound as if you could go to a store and buy a woman."

"Sometimes I wish it were that simple." Houston crossed to a window and stared out. "Not all of us have real jobs and stay in one location where we could meet a girl the regular way, take the time to woo her and fall in love. I rarely get to a second date, because it seems I'm deployed before I can call one back."

"Speaking of dates..." Adam cornered Dustin. "How'd it go with the news reporter last night?"

"Yeah," Houston grinned. "Did you make headlines?"

Dustin didn't want to talk about it, but his brothers wouldn't let him off the hook lightly. "It was all right."

"What? Just all right? You didn't get to her with the Ford Charm?"

Adam shook his head. "You didn't come back to the

ranch, so either she didn't kick you out or you went to a hotel. Which was it?"

Dustin glared at his brothers. "None of your business."

Houston gave Adam a knowing look. "As grumpy as he is, I'd say he spent the night in a hotel room."

"What does it matter where I spent the night? Things between me and Jenna aren't going to amount to anything," Dustin insisted. "Like Houston said, what woman will put up with a man who's gone ninety-nine percent of the time and is being shot at or having rockets fired at him while he's hovering helplessly above the ground in a tin can?"

"A strong woman who cares enough about the man to be there when he gets back." Dustin's mother's voice sounded behind him.

He spun to face her. "Mom, it's not worth trying. It won't work."

"What did you say before?" She tapped her finger to her chin. "Ah, yes. You can do anything you set your mind to."

"Except make someone love you enough to be there when you get back." Dustin's lips twisted. "Hell, she didn't even wait until I left to ditch me last time. She dumped me before I left."

"Did you ask her why?" his mother demanded.

What was with his mother's relentless determination to dig into his past? "She told me she didn't want to be tied down."

Her eyes narrowed. "She didn't want to be tied down, or she didn't want you to be tied down?"

Dustin shrugged. "It's the same thing."

His mother crossed her arms. "Would you have gone on to become a SEAL if she hadn't told you it was over?"

"Hell, no. I'd have married her and we'd have a couple kids by now."

His mother's lips curved into a gentle smile. "You dreamed about being a SEAL from the moment you watched a show about them on television when you were only six years old. When the Navy made the offer for you to enlist and go straight into the SEAL training program, you were beyond excited."

"Because it got me away from here. Away from Jenna."

"If I recall, you got that offer after you proposed to Jenna, and before she broke it off." His mother rolled her eyes. "Didn't you question the timing? I'll lay you odds, Jenna knew you were selected for SEAL training when she broke your engagement. Are you sure she doesn't love you?"

His mother was headed down the wrong path. Jenna didn't love him. "She threw my ring back in my face."

"Where is that ring now?" His mother's brows rose.

"How should I know?" He ran a hand through his hair, ignoring the smirks on his brothers' faces. "I told her I didn't give a damn about the ring. She could keep it, sell it, or throw it away. She probably threw it away."

"Did you ask her what she did with it?"

"Why? It's old news. She was done with me ten years ago."

"Then why did she invite you to stay at her place in town?" Dustin's mother was like a bulldog with a bone in her mouth and she wasn't letting go.

"She was just being nice."

Both Adam and Houston snorted, but kept their comments to themselves. Apparently they were enjoying his discomfort at his mother's grilling.

"Uh huh." His mother clucked her tongue. "You can be as dense and stubborn as your father." She raised her hands when Dustin opened his mouth to protest. "But you know best, and you've had so much experience reading women's minds." She filled her coffee cup and turned to leave, pausing before she stepped out of the waiting room. "Are you going to let her get away again, or are you going to fight for something you really, really want."

"I don't want Jenna." Dustin threw his hands in the air. "Just because I slept with the woman doesn't mean I want to pick up where we left off. It was sex. Only sex."

"I knew it!" Houston exclaimed.

"No, you didn't." Always the level head, Adam touched Dustin's arm. "If you don't want her in your life, don't go back to her apartment. Come home to the ranch tonight."

"I will," Dustin said, convinced this was the only way to prove to his brothers he wasn't interested in pursuing Jenna. Damn. He'd left his duffle bag at her apartment.

He fingered the key in his pocket. He could go by her place during the day, hopefully while she was at work, and collect his belongings.

"Yeah. I won't hold my breath." Houston pulled a twenty out of his wallet and held it up to Adam. "Twenty says he won't be at the ranch tonight."

Adam snorted. "Can't bet against you, man. I'm of the same opinion."

Dustin turned and followed his mother down the hall to where his father lay sleeping. "Mom, why don't you go home, get a shower and rest? You look exhausted. I'll stay with Dad today."

Her brow puckered. "Do you think he'll mind? I could use a shower. I can be back in a couple hours."

"Take the day and sleep in your own bed. Or, better yet, let me stay with him tonight."

"No one needs to stay with me," his father said, his voice more like a croak than his normal rich timbre. "I'm not a baby."

"You don't have a say in this," Dustin's mother said with the firmness she'd used on her sons when they were small. "I'm going home for a shower and a nap, but I'll be back tonight."

"You should go home and stay. I can manage on my own."

"What part of you don't have a say in this, did you not understand?" Jeannie Ford slipped her purse strap over her shoulder. "Now, behave yourself when the nurses come in. No pinching and no harassing them. They're here to help you."

"Yes, ma'am." His father's lips quirked. "Should have been a drill sergeant, not just a housewife."

"Mr. Ford, if you ever call me just a housewife again, I swear you'll regret it." She bent and kissed his cheek. "I'll be back. I love you, even if you do try my patience."

As Dustin's mother stalked out of the room, his father made a soft chuffing sound Dustin realized was an attempt to chuckle, followed by a wince. He rested one of his hands on his chest. "Damn, that hurts. Tell that confounded woman I'm a sick man, and I don't need her stirring me up or making me laugh."

A nurse came in, checked his vital signs and the tube draining his chest. She put a different device in his mouth and asked him to blow into it. He did, though it was a weak attempt.

Dustin had never seen his father so helpless, and it shook him to his core.

When the nurse left, the older Ford's eyelids drifted closed. "Do me a favor, will ya?" he said.

"Anything."

"Go away and let me sleep."

Dustin smiled. "You're going to be all right, Dad."

"Damn right I am."

Adam met him at the door. "Houston is driving Mom home. I'll take over here, if you have something else you want to do."

"I do have an errand to run, but I don't have to be gone long."

"Go. I've got this covered," Adam said. "You might want to stop in the waiting room and check out the television. Jenna was on the news when I left. You might catch her report on the local children's shelter.

"I'll be back soon." Dustin sauntered out of the CICU room, feigning indifference to what his brother had said about Jenna. As soon as he cleared the door, he practically hustled to the waiting room where he caught the tail end of Jenna's segment about the local children.

She sat cross-legged in the middle of a room full of small children, all vying for a spot in her lap. One little girl wrapped her arms around Jenna's neck and kissed her.

Jenna laughed, smiling into the camera. "Be sure to attend the benefit for the shelter. These children need your help." She laid down her microphone and hugged the little girl, her eyes shining.

The image of Jenna with the little girls and boys tugged hard on Dustin's heart. She'd make a great mother.

With Jenna laughing and smiling on the screen, Dustin found himself wanting more out of life than only his work as a SEAL. He wanted a woman to come home to and children to spoil.

He stared at the screen until the image of a laughing Jenna disappeared, replaced by a sales ad for new cars.

Being home and surrounded by his family reminded

him of what a great childhood he'd had and the exciting times he'd had with Jenna, racing horses across the pastures, swimming naked in the creek and making love beneath the stars. He'd been certain she was the one.

If he went after her again, he chanced having his heart broken all over again. If he didn't go after her, would she be one of his big regrets? Dustin had learned that regrets stemmed from things he didn't do, not from those he attempted and failed.

He'd go by her apartment to collect his bag. If she was there, he'd take her lead and see where it went, see whether their relationship was actually going anywhere. If she wasn't there, he'd take his bag and go home.

As he stepped out of the hospital into the hot Texas sunshine pounding down on him, he found himself hoping she'd be there.

7

J enna had been bucking for the high-intensity stories, hoping to capture the attention of the major news networks and maybe landing a job in a town bigger than Waco. But she refused to give up coverage of one of her favorite non-profit events. The fundraiser for the local children's shelter was something she volunteered for every year.

Waking to an empty bed, after a night of mind-blowing sex, had started her day with the disappointing conclusion she'd struck out on luring Dustin back to her side. Sure they'd had great sex, but it hadn't made him want to stick around.

Her only hope lay in the fact he'd left his duffle bag on the floor in her living room. He had to come back for it, and when he did, she hoped she'd be there to tempt him into her bed for one more night. If she played her cards right, they'd have repeat performances through the week and by the time he had to report back to his unit, he'd realize he still loved her and wanted to be with her for the rest of his life.

Yeah, and pigs fly.

Toby packed up his camera, while Jenna said goodbye to the children.

Together, they walked out to the parking lot. The hot sun beat down on Jenna, draining her energy.

"Could it get any hotter?" Toby pushed a hand through his shaggy hair, beads of sweat popping out on his forehead.

"The weatherman was right when he said we were in for a dry summer. We could sure use a good drenching rain to refill the reservoirs."

"I hear the prairie fire they're fighting northwest of town has consumed six hundred acres already."

"What prairie fire?" Jenna shook off her heat-induced lethargy. "Why didn't you say something earlier?"

"I thought you would have heard about it on the police scanner." Her cousin shrugged. "Besides, you always cover the children's shelter fundraiser. They sent Steve to cover the fire this morning."

"Damn. Fires get national attention." Jenna's shoulders slumped. "But you're right. I wouldn't miss covering the fundraiser for the kids." She pulled her phone out of her purse and checked her text messages. "I'm worried about Rebecca."

"Have you heard from her since yesterday?"

"No. I'm worried they might have found her cell phone."

"I wish you could have talked her out of going back."

"I couldn't. She wouldn't leave her mother there."

"Any mother who'd get her daughter involved in something like that should have her head examined."

"For all outward appearances, they're a peaceful community, sharing the fruits of their labors."

"Then why the high walls, fences and tight rules? To me, it spells fanatics and brainwashing."

"I'm with you." She tapped her finger to her chin, sweat dripping between her breasts. "I need to get in there and see for myself what's going on."

"Is she supposed to be at the farmer's market today?"

"I think so. I'll check it out." And if she wasn't there, Jenna would have to get inside the compound and figure out what was going on.

"Oh, no." Toby laid a hand on her arm. "I see that look in your eyes. Don't do anything stupid, Jenna."

She smiled up at him, innocently. "I don't know what you're talking about."

"If you do anything, call me. You'll need me to film for evidence."

"You're on. Now get out of here before we both cook in our shoes." She climbed into her SUV and switched the AC to full blast. Damn it was hot.

Her first stop would be her apartment to see if Dustin had been back to collect his duffle. She'd grab the pale green gingham dress Rebecca had gifted her with when she'd first learned to sew at the compound. If she had to get into the compound, she'd blend in better if she were dressed like the others.

At her apartment, she stared around the parking lot. There were a few cars parked there and one SUV. She didn't even know what Dustin was driving. He could be in her apartment and she wouldn't know it until she stepped through the door.

Her pulse quickened and she flew up the stairs, crossing her fingers as she twisted the key in the lock. Taking a deep breath, she pushed the door open.

Sun edged through the half-closed blinds, but no other lights were on, the living room was empty, and a quick check in the bedroom and bathroom proved they were empty, too. The good news was the duffle bag was still where Dustin had left it that morning.

Her heart fluttered at the sight of the bag. She wanted to hide it in her closet in case he came to collect the bag while she was out. It would force him to return when she was there.

She grabbed the handles of the bag and was halfway to her bedroom closet when she stopped. Hiding it would be too desperate. If Dustin wanted to collect it without running into her, that was his choice. It would put the kibosh on her attempt to seduce him into her bed for a second night of mattress dancing.

Jenna hugged the bag to her chest, tears pooling in her eyes. It smelled of canvas and outdoors, with the faint aroma of Dustin's aftershave. For the millionth time in the past ten years, she questioned her decision to break their engagement. From all accounts, he'd become the best SEAL a man could want to be, defending the country's freedom, rescuing citizens trapped in foreign countries and taking down the bad guys. If she hadn't set him free, he might have come to resent her and their marriage. At the least, he'd have lived with regret for not having attempted to make it as a SEAL.

No. She'd made the right choice.

Metal scraped in the lock on the door to her apartment and the knob twisted.

Jenna flung the duffle bag onto the floor where she'd found it as the door opened.

Dustin entered, his gaze sweeping the room, landing on her. His nostrils flared and he froze.

Heat traveled up Jenna's neck and into her cheeks at almost getting caught holding his bag.

His broad shoulders filled the doorway, stretching the fabric of his T-shirt across the well-defined muscles.

The fire burning in Jenna's cheeks spread south as memories of lying naked in her bed with this man washed over her. She swallowed hard and forced a greeting past her dry lips. "Hey."

Dustin stepped through the door and closed it behind him, but didn't move to lessen the distance between them. "Hey, yourself."

Jenna pointed to the bag on the floor. "Are you here for your bag?"

He nodded.

"You can leave it here for the week, if you want." Yeah, she was sounding pretty damned desperate. What she really wanted to say was, Please, stay with me for the week and forever. As much as she wanted to be with him, she couldn't expose herself to that extent. He'd made it perfectly clear making love to her didn't mean anything. Her heart pinched in her chest, making it hard for her to breathe.

Dustin took one step forward, his gaze capturing hers. "Why did you invite me to stay with you?"

She glanced away first. "I didn't see a need for you...or your family...to pay for a hotel room when I live close enough."

"And that's the only reason?" He took two more steps, his stride long enough to eat up the distance between the door and her.

Her heart pounded, sending blood rushing to her head, the sound blasting against her eardrums. Had he figured out that she'd planned all along to seduce him? "No o-other r-reason. Why do you ask?"

He caught her chin in his grip and raised her face, forcing her to look into his eyes. "Why did you break up with me ten years ago?"

"We were too young," she said, a sob rising up to block her vocal cords.

He slid his hand behind her head and bent, his lips hovering over hers. "Bullshit."

"I wanted to pursue my career," she whispered.

"Does it keep you warm at night?"

She shook her head, her gaze shifting to his where she fell into his dark eyes, drowning in her longing to be held by this man.

His grip tightened. "I don't know what's happening between us, or if it has staying power, but, damn it, I can't walk away. Not yet."

The warmth of his breath on her lips made her body tingle from head to toe and she swayed toward him. "Then don't," she whispered and lifted up on the balls of her feet, sealing her lips over his.

His fingers twisted in her hair, tilting her head back as she deepened the kiss, ravaging her mouth with his tongue.

Jenna wrapped her arms around his middle and held on, afraid her knees would buckle if she let go.

This was where she wanted to be, where she belonged. For ten long years, she'd dreamed of the day he would come home and call her bluff. And here he was, holding her like he might never let her go. Heaven must have been smiling down on her.

He swept his hands down her back and pressed them against the backs of her thighs, lifting her.

Jenna wrapped her legs around his waist, her breasts smashed against his hard chest.

Dustin backed her up against the wall increasing the pressure on her mouth, the hard ridge beneath his fly pressing into Jenna's crotch.

She threaded her fingers in his hair and held him close, savoring the taste, look and feel of him, committing this time together to her memories. If he walked away at the end of the day or the week, she'd have no regrets for having tried to win back his heart.

Dustin pinned Jenna to the wall, raising her hands above her head, trapping them with one of his, and keeping her from touching him as he plundered her lips. An animalistic urge to stake his claim and take what he wanted washed over him, ten years of longing for her rising in him in a wave of anger at being cheated out of all those years of loving her. Yanking her away from the wall, he turned and draped her across the brown leather couch, scattering bright pillows across the floor.

He attacked her lips and cheeks, trailing nibbles and kisses down the long line of her neck and lower to the swell of her breasts beneath her crisp white blouse. She writhed beneath him, working at the hem of his T-shirt, trying to pull it up his torso, while he tugged at the buttons on her shirt, popping a few when he grew frustrated with the tiny buttons.

Jenna covered his hand with hers. "Let me, before you ruin my shirt."

Dustin moved his hand, and Jenna managed the buttons in half the time, shrugging out of the shirt's sleeves. With Jenna's help, Dustin had her skirt off in record time.

She lay on the couch in nothing but a white lace bra and thong panties. "A little overdressed, are you?" Jenna's brows rose in challenge.

Ripping his shirt over his head, Dustin tossed it

across the room, and then he stood and yanked the button on his fly.

Jenna sat up and reached for the tab on his zipper, easing it slowly down, her tongue sliding across her lips, doing funny things to Dustin's insides.

When she had the zip down, his cock, hard as steel, sprang out.

Jenna captured it in her palms and rubbed her cheek along its length. Then she turned and swept her tongue over the rounded head.

Dustin dug his fingers into her thick auburn hair and urged her closer.

She licked him again, this time circling the tip.

He groaned, his buttocks tightening, blood rushing to his groin.

"Like that?" she asked, her breath warm across the damp area she'd just licked. In her next breath, she wrapped her lips around his length and sucked him into her mouth. She dug her fingers into his buttocks, hauling him closer, scraping her teeth lightly along his length.

Electric current raced from his cock throughout his body, rippling in waves of sensation all the way to his extremities. He closed his eyes, dragging in a ragged breath as he eased out of her mouth and back in. She pressed hard on his ass, forcing him to glide deep, until he bumped against the back of her throat.

His control shattered, and he pumped in and out of her mouth, anchoring his hands in her hair.

The faster he went, the hotter he grew, igniting a

passionate flame that sent him spiraling to the top. Just before he launched, he jerked free of her mouth, and sucked in a lungful of air.

"Protection," she said, through swollen lips. She caught her bottom lip between her teeth, unhooked her bra and slid her panties down her legs.

Lust firing his neurons, Dustin dove for his jeans, removed his wallet from his back pocket and flipped through until he found a foil package. Tossing the wallet aside, he tore open the envelope and slid the condom over his throbbing cock.

Holding tight to his release, he flipped Jenna on her stomach.

She squealed in surprise and tried to rise up on her hands.

Before she could, he gripped her hips and raised her bottom into the air. In the next second, he drove into her from behind.

Her fingers curled into the couch cushion, a moan rising from her throat.

Her smooth white bottom tempted the saint out of him and he slapped it, leaving a light pink mark on her skin.

"Oh!" Jenna flinched.

He smoothed his hand over the pink imprint. "Did I hurt you?"

"No." She chuckled. "You surprised me."

"Do you want me to do it again?"

"Yes, please." She arched her back, presenting her ass

for his pleasure and he complied, popping her again with a light smack that was more noise than pain.

"Mmm. Yes!" Planting her face on the seat cushion, she reached ran her hand between her legs and fondled him, rolling his balls between her fingers.

Dustin bent over her back and cupped her breasts, settling into a fast, steady rhythm, building tension until he rocketed into the heavens. He straightened, grabbed her hips and thrust one last time, holding himself deep, deep, deep inside her, his cock throbbing, pulsing with his release.

Minutes later, he pulled free, shifted her legs off the couch and sat, dragging her across his lap.

She lay nestled against him. "Even better than when we were kids learning how to fit part A into slot B."

"You're amazing."

Jenna laid her cheek against his chest. "Your heart is racing."

"You do that to me," he murmured.

She leaned up and kissed him, her mouth musky with the scent of him.

Again, she rested her cheek against his chest, her fingers toying with one of his hard brown nipples. "Is there any future for us?"

He didn't answer, afraid if he said yes, she'd contradict him telling him she wasn't in it for the long haul.

Jenna sighed. "It doesn't matter. We have this moment. That will be enough for now."

Across the room, a cell phone dinged, announcing a text message.

Jenna's fingers stilled on his nipple and she raised up, her brows knitting.

"Let it go."

She shook her head, pushing off him to rise to her feet, glancing from him to the cell phone. "I can't let it go." Jenna hurried to her purse on the kitchen counter, yanked out her phone and read the text. Her lips thinned and she tucked the phone back in her purse. "I have to leave." Without looking him in the eye, she gathered her panties and bra, left her skirt and shirt on the floor and ran for her room.

Dustin rose from the couch, dragged on his jeans and boots.

Before he could find his shirt, Jenna emerged from her bedroom dressed in black jeans, a black shirt and tennis shoes. She carried a bag stuffed with what looked like a wad of light green and white fabric. As she reached the door, she turned. "Will you be here all night?"

His lips pressed into a line. "Not if you aren't."

She nodded. "I understand."

He reached out a hand. "Stay with me."

For a long moment, she stared at that hand, and then she shook her head. "I have to go."

Dustin didn't try to stop her again.

Jenna left the apartment, closing the door softly behind her.

Dustin waited, hoping she'd change her mind. When

the door remained closed, he yanked the T-shirt over his head, strode to the door and yanked it open.

Jenna's black SUV pulled out of the parking lot and onto the street.

So much for their loving reunion. He'd offered to stay. She'd refused. End of story.

Dustin gathered his duffle bag, dropped her apartment key on the table by the door, walked out of Jenna's apartment and stomped down the stairs to climb into his rental. As soon as he closed the door, he regretted his anger and his knee-jerk reaction to Jenna leaving him. What if the text had been an emergency? What if someone she knew was in trouble?

Dustin rested his forehead against the steering wheel. Damn.

Why couldn't he do things right the first time? If Jenna came back to her apartment, found his bag gone and the key on the table, she'd jump to the conclusion he'd intended.

Only now, he wished he hadn't done it. How in hell was he going to convince her he wasn't through—that he wanted to continue their relationship to the end of the week and longer. He'd have his work cut out for him.

First, he needed to check in at the hospital. Then he had to find Jenna.

8

J enna called Toby as she sped toward the farmer's market.

"Damn, Jenna, I was sound asleep, dreaming about a big beautiful...uh, pepperoni pizza. Just when I was about to take a bite, you called. Way to kill a great dream." He yawned into the phone. "What's up?"

"Rebecca contacted me."

"Why didn't you say so in the first place?"

She snorted softly. "You were too busy complaining. I'm meeting her at the farmer's market. Can you get there in the next fifteen minutes?"

"I can. Bring the camera?"

"Yes and no," Jenna said.

"Huh?"

"I know you have one of those mini cameras." Jenna slowed her car and turned at a corner. "Bring it."

"Please tell me you're not going to infiltrate the

compound," Toby moaned.

"Okay, I won't tell you. Just bring the mini-cam."

"What will I tell your mother if you don't come out?"

Jenna snorted. "My mother's in China with husband number four. She won't care."

"Well, I do," Toby grumbled. "I'm going with you."

"You can't. You don't have the clothing they wear."

"And you do?" Her cousin snorted. "I've seen those baggy dresses. I don't picture you wearing one."

"Rebecca made one for me last year. It'll help me blend in with the others."

"Darlin', it's a small community. Everyone knows everyone else. They'll notice you."

"I'll wear one of those bonnets. It's hot and sunny outside. I've seen them wear them to the market."

Toby paused and then said, "I don't like it."

"I don't like it anymore than you do. I could be back at my apartment in the arms of the man I love. Instead, I'm chasing after family members who've made some poor choices."

"You and the SEAL got it on?" Toby chuckled. "Good for you."

"It's only good if it lasts more than this week."

"You're a babe. He can't help falling in love with you."

Jenna wished that was true. With a family member in crisis, she didn't have time to test the theory. If all went well, she'd get into the compound tonight, find out what they were hiding and get Rebecca and her mother out of there before the sun rose. And if the elders were hiding something illegal, she'd wait until they were all safe before she turned the police, sheriff or ATF loose on them.

With a shorter distance to go, she pulled into a parking space near the farmer's market and got out. The hot sun broiled her in the black T-shirt and jeans she wore. She almost regretted her choice, but she'd wanted to come prepared for covert operations, whether she would be moving through the shadows of night or playing the chameleon and blending in with the residents of Sweet Salvation.

Jenna glanced at the sky. The white-hot sun shone down on the market. A cloud flitted by and several more gathered in the western sky. She could only hope they would form into rain clouds. Sneaking into the compound would be easier under the cover of a storm.

But then, this was Texas in the late summer. It could go months without a drop of rain, or it could rain so hard in one hour it would cause flooding. She'd seen the Brazos River rise so high it covered bridges and pushed entire trees over.

She wandered through the booths with their tents erected to shade their occupants from the sun. The Sweet Salvation booth was at the far end of the market. When Jenna was close enough to make out faces of the women manning the booth, she didn't find Rebecca's among them.

Jenna's cell phone vibrated in her back pocket. She pulled it out and turned her back to the women in gingham and calico dresses and read the message from Toby.

I'm here, where are you?

She responded and walked back the way she came. When she spotted Toby, she pulled him behind a stand selling kettle corn.

Toby's brows furrowed. "I really don't like that you're thinking about going in. We have no idea what they'll do to you."

"Relax. They're supposed to be peace-loving and benevolent."

"Didn't you tell me Rebecca reported that they were whipped when they didn't follow the rules?"

"That's the people in the cult. I'm not a member. If I'm found, they'll just escort me to the gate and boot my ass out." She hoped her self-assured statement would satisfy her cousin, even though it sounded pretty weak to her.

Toby shook his head, dug in his pocket and pulled out a miniscule mini-camcorder. "You press this little button on the back when you want to record. If you have it pinned on your person, you can smash your hand over it and it will depress the button against your skin."

Jenna slipped the device into her pocket.

Toby handed her a flat metal disk. "Stick this in your bra."

She held the disk up and studied it. "What is it?"

"A GPS tracker. I have a handheld gizmo that will find this little bad boy anywhere."

"I'm going to the compound, not the jungles of

Central America."

"Just put it in your bra. If I don't hear from you by morning, I want to be able to find you."

She smiled. "I'll wear it, but I doubt it'll be as bad as all that. Like I said, if they discover me, they'll likely march me to the gate—at which point, I'll call you on my cell phone."

"If they don't confiscate it, and if they don't lock you in a basement where no one will hear your screams."

A shiver rippled down her spine. She'd made light of being caught to spare Toby from worry. Yet, the whole reason she was going in to the compound was because she feared for Rebecca's and her mother's lives. Some cult leaders were sociopathic nut jobs, looking for the moment to light up the powder keg. Hell, it had happened before with David Koresh and his brainwashed minions. Many lives had been lost, putting Waco on the map as an example of how ATF should not storm a compound full of women and children and crazy cult leaders.

Jenna hoped she wasn't blowing Rebecca's troubles out of proportion and that the teen was over-exaggerating what was going on inside the Sweet Salvation community.

Tucking the GPS tag into her bra, she met Toby's gaze. "I'll be all right. I'm just going in to help Rebecca convince her mother to leave with us. Can you be on standby when we come out? We'll need transportation back into town."

"You bet." Toby touched her arm. "Jenna, don't try to be a hero. If Rebecca's mother won't come out, grab Rebecca and get yourself out before sunrise."

She nodded.

"Promise me," Toby insisted.

As scared as Rebecca was, she hadn't left the Sweet Salvation community, making Jenna think bringing Rebecca out would be completely contingent on getting her mother out as well. If all else failed, Jenna might come out alone, but at least she'd have answers about what was really going on behind the compound fences and walls. "Okay. I promise."

Toby's lips pressed together. "I have a bad feeling about this, but I know how you are."

Jenna laughed. "How's that?"

"Like a bull dog with a bone in his mouth. You won't let go until you get to the bottom of it."

"I know my limits," she countered.

"Yeah, sure." He pointed to the bandage on her temple barely covered by her hair. "You know your limits."

She raised a hand halfway to her injury. "How was I supposed to know he'd get out and start shooting so erratically?"

"Exactly," Toby said. "You can't predict how or when a situation is going to go south." He pulled her into his arms and hugged her tight. "I like having my cousin around. Keep your head down and stay away from trouble."

She hugged him back then pushed away from him. "I'll be fine," she said with more certainty than she felt. Sliding the bag with her dress over her shoulder, she patted her bra where the GPS disc nestled and touched the pocket with the mini-cam. Setting her cell phone on silent, she was ready. "Wish me luck."

"I feel like I should say break a leg."

"Whatever." Jenna kissed his cheek and left him behind the kettle corn stand while she pretended to shop one booth to the next, working her way toward the Sweet Salvation booth. It was almost time for the vendors to pack up for the day. She paused in front of a rack of bonnets and selected one that would go with her dress, handing over a twenty. Rebecca straightened from behind the booth, a box of jams and jellies in her arms. Her eyes flared and her face flushed. Her gaze darted around to the older women. Thankfully, they were busy packing their wares into other boxes.

Rebecca tilted her head just enough to indicate Jenna should follow, but not enough to draw attention from the others.

Jenna tucked her bonnet into her bag, smiled and walked past several booths before ducking between two and making her way back to where Rebecca had headed. She found her rearranging the boxes, watching out of the corners of her eyes for any movement.

When Jenna reached her, she yanked her down behind the tailgate.

"Something's going down at the community," Rebecca

whispered.

"What?"

"Last night, the men were called into a meeting that lasted well past midnight."

"So?"

"Late yesterday afternoon, I was out at the garden and heard the sounds of gunfire. Lots of gunfire. It sounded like a war zone, but at specific intervals."

"Like target practice?"

Rebecca nodded. "I tried to get my mother to come with me today. We could have walked away from the market and no one would have been able to stop us. But she wouldn't come. She won't listen to me and thinks everything is fine."

"Sounds to me like it isn't. Why would a peaceful commune need to learn how to fire guns?"

"My exact thought." Rebecca's brows puckered. "I could understand, if it were for hunting, but then why would all the men be missing when they should have been plowing, fixing fences or building stuff?"

"Have you seen Rebecca?" a female voice called out.

Rebecca ducked lower. "I have to get back to work or they'll come looking for me."

"I'm coming with you when you leave," Jenna said. "Maybe I can make your mother see that it's not safe at Sweet Salvation."

Her cousin shook her head. "No, no, you can't. They don't allow strangers on the compound."

Jenna smiled. "I'm not asking permission. I'll stow

away in the back of one of the trucks."

"I don't know what to do about that girl," the woman said. "Every time I turn around, she disappears."

"Should we tell the elders?" another voice asked.

"No, no. You and I will take care of it."

The other woman snorted. "When we find her."

Jenna lowered her voice to a soft whisper. "Distract them while I climb in."

"But—"

"Shh." Jenna pressed her finger to her lips.

"Do you need help getting that box in the back of the truck?" a woman's voice said and the shuffle of feet sounded on the pavement.

Jenna laid down on her back and rolled beneath the truck.

Rebecca straightened.

"There you are," the woman said. "Here. Take this box and stack it with the others. Rose and Martha are bringing the booth. Leave room for it."

"Yes, ma'am." Rebecca's feet left the ground as she climbed up into the back of the truck.

Jenna lay beneath the truck counting pairs of shoes as the women loaded their boxes into the back. Two more pairs of serviceable tennis shoes appeared, and the women hefted the booth into the back of the truck, the wooden platform clanging against the metal bed.

"Just a few more boxes and we can leave," the lead woman said. "Rebecca, you can start covering the boxes with the tarp so that the sun doesn't cook the jelly."

"Yes, ma'am."

All four pair of feet walked back toward the farmer's market. The sound of Rebecca shifting items in the truck bed was followed by the rustle of canvas. Then Rebecca jumped to the ground at the tailgate and bent to peer beneath the vehicle. "If you're determined to do this, you better get moving now."

Jenna rolled from beneath the truck and came up on her haunches.

Rebecca straightened, glancing over the top of truck. "You can crawl beneath the tarp. I made a hole between the boxes of jam and jelly. It's small, but I think you can fit." She continued to stare over the truck. "Hurry, they'll be back any minute."

Jenna climbed into the back of the truck, staying low to avoid being seen and settled into the gap between boxes.

"Here they come." Rebecca dragged the tarp over Jenna and the boxes.

"This is the last of it," the lead woman said.

"Set them on the tailgate. I'll stack them," Rebecca offered, climbing into the bed again.

Wedged between boxes and buried beneath a heavy tarp, Jenna tugged at her shirt. Sweat beaded on her forehead and dripped down between her breasts. She prayed they'd get moving soon or she'd die of heatstroke before she made it to Sweet Salvation.

Rebecca arranged the boxes and secured the corners of the tarp to the metal anchors in the bed of the truck.

When she was done, she jumped down, the truck bed rising slightly. The tailgate slammed and the next sound Jenna heard was the truck's door closing after Rebecca climbed into the cab. A moment later the engine started, and the driver backed out of the parking space. Not until they'd made it out of downtown Waco did the truck's motion speed up enough to get air flowing beneath the tarp.

Hot and exhausted, Jenna's eyes drifted closed.

Damn it. Jenna shook her head, forcing her eyes open in the dim light. She couldn't go to sleep, even if she hadn't slept much the night before. Too much was dependent on her staying fully alert. The truck bumped along. The heat and the rocking motion worked against her and she drifted off before reaching the compound.

DUSTIN SPENT most of the afternoon with his father, who was getting grouchier by the minute and feeling the pain set in from having his ribs cracked open and his heart worked on. No amount of cheering pleased the man, but he had a right to be petulant after what he'd gone through.

"Go," Dustin's mother said when she returned from the ranch, having showered, slept for four hours and had dinner. She looked rested, less stressed and ready to spend the night in the room with her husband. "Go," she repeated. "Get some rest."

Rest was the farthest thing from his mind. When the

nurses had been in and out of his father's room, Dustin had stepped out into the hallway and called around trying to locate Jenna.

Her boss at the television station hadn't heard from her since that morning's fund raising event. Each time Dustin called her cell phone, he got her voicemail. He tried finding Toby's number, but it was unlisted.

When his mother told him to go, he didn't hesitate. He drove straight to Jenna's apartment and ran up the steps. He knocked and waited, his breath caught in his lungs. She didn't answer the door, and he couldn't see any lights shining through the blinds. Just in case she'd gone to sleep, he knocked louder.

Nothing stirred behind the door.

With nowhere else to turn, he headed for the news station. They would be gearing up for the evening news and weather. Someone had to be there who might have an alternate cell phone number for Jenna or Toby's number.

The front door of the news station was locked.

Reaching the end of his patience, Dustin considered breaking the glass door and charging in.

"Are you looking for someone?" a voice sounded behind him.

Dustin turned toward a tall blonde he vaguely recognized as one of the station's anchors. "I'm trying to find Jenna Turner."

"Are you a friend or a stalker fan?" The blonde winked.

"Fiancé." The word rolled off his tongue like it belonged.

The blonde's brows rose. "I didn't know Jenna was engaged."

"I've been out of town."

The woman's gaze raked over him from head to toe. "I can see why she didn't want to share. She won the sexy fiancé lottery when she landed you." She stuck out her hand. "I'm Ashlynn Grant. Jenna usually isn't in the studio at this time."

"I know. I'm trying to find her, but she isn't answering her cell phone. I've been by her apartment and she's not at home."

"Is something wrong?"

"I'm not sure. I haven't heard from her all day, and I'm concerned." It wasn't a lie. The darker the sky grew, the more worried he became.

"Have you called her cousin Toby? If they're following a story, he'll be with her."

"I just got back into town, I don't have his number, and it's unlisted."

Ashlynn pulled her cell phone from her purse and scrolled through her contacts. "Here it is. He and Jenna are my go-to people for freelance reporting. They're not afraid of anything, and they always do a great job."

Dustin entered the number into his cell phone. Before he hit SEND, he nodded to Ashlynn. "Thanks."

"Anytime," she said and unlocked the front door, letting herself into the station.

Before the door closed behind Ashlynn, Dustin hit the SEND key and waited for someone to answer on the other end.

"This is Toby."

"Toby, Dustin Ford. I'm looking for Jenna. Do you know where I can find her?"

"Uh..." Toby said and paused.

"She might be mad at me and not want to talk, but I need to tell her something important." Dustin wasn't above begging. "Please."

"I don't know anything about her being mad at you, but I don't know if she'd want me to tell you where she is."

Dustin walked back to the SUV he'd rented and leaned against the front grill. "Look, I don't know why she's not answering her phone, but I have to talk to her. Damn it, I love her and I don't want to leave Texas without telling her."

"I'd love to get her on the line for you to do just that, but she's actually on assignment."

"She's working?" Dustin's grip tightened on the phone. "She's not covering another shoot out, is she?"

"Not that I know of..." Toby hedged.

"You're not with her?"

"No," Toby's said, his voice tight, strained. "And I'm not happy about it."

"Toby, if she's in trouble, tell me."

"I don't know if she is or not." Toby sighed. "Hell, I

might as well tell you. If something goes south, you might be able to help her more than the authorities."

Dustin wasn't liking the sound of this. "Where is she?" he asked, his tone deep, insistent. He wished he could reach through the phone and drag the information out of Toby.

"She's going to infiltrate the Sweet Salvation community. If all went well, she should be inside the compound now."

Dustin's heart dropped to the bottom of belly. "Isn't that the religious commune outside of town?"

"Yes."

"I thought they were all about peace, love and acceptance."

"As long as you accept that you live by their rules, accept their punishments and don't look behind the curtain," Toby said. "Our cousin Rebecca joined the commune last year." Toby filled Dustin in on how Rebecca had reached out to Jenna in her fear for herself and her mother. He told him she'd seen them bringing in wooden crates into the worship center, and then stowing them in the basement.

"So?"

"The elders are being very secretive, and Rebecca is concerned they're doing something illegal. Jenna wanted Rebecca to get out if she was uncomfortable with what was going on, but Rebecca refused to leave her mother who's also a member of the group."

"And Jenna is going in to convince Rebecca and her mother to leave with her?" Dustin asked.

"That and to figure out what the elders are hiding in the basement of the worship hall," Toby concluded.

Dustin scrubbed a hand down his face. What the hell had Jenna gotten herself into? "What was her plan?"

"She's supposed to call me before morning to come pick her up on the highway outside the compound. If she's successful, she'll have Rebecca and her mother with her. Otherwise she'll be on her own."

"If she gets out without being detected," Dustin muttered.

"Hey, I'm not any happier about this than you are. I gave her a mini-cam to video what she finds and a GPS tracking tag, so I can at least locate her."

"You put a tracker on her?"

"Hell, yeah. She's going into that crazy place. No telling what'll happen."

Dustin's thought, exactly. The last time a commune in the Waco area was challenged, a lot of people died. He didn't want that to happen again. Not with Jenna inside.

"Text me your address. I'll be by to pick you up in fifteen minutes," Dustin said.

"And do what?" Toby asked.

"We're going to the compound."

"They won't let us in."

Dustin's hand tightened on the cell phone. "My brothers and I don't need an invitation."

9

The truck jerked to a stop, slamming Jenna against the stack of boxes, waking her. She held her breath and listened to the sounds of a gate opening and male voices speaking to the female driver.

Sweating, hot and nervous, she remained quiet and still. If the gatekeepers chose to look under the tarp, it would be all too easy to see her, and they'd refuse to allow her into the compound. They would accuse Rebecca of hiding her among the boxes of jams and jellies. If they were whipping cult members for infractions, they'd turn their whips loose on Rebecca, and Jenna couldn't let that happen.

A minute passed with the gatekeeper chatting with the driver, and then the truck shifted into drive and pulled forward, off the paved road.

Jenna let out the breath she'd held the entire time.

For the next five minutes, they bumped over what sounded like a gravel road. The truck slowed to a stop, the screech of unoiled hinges sounded and the truck moved forward slowly, coming to a halt. The faint light that had found its way through and around the tarp had diminished to near-darkness. The truck doors opened and closed, the women talking as they walked away.

"Aren't you coming with us, Rebecca?" a woman asked.

"I want to load a few more boxes into the truck for tomorrow's market so that we don't have to do it in the morning."

"We'll save you a plate at the dinner table. Don't take too long, or you'll be late for worship."

"I'll hurry," Rebecca responded.

The squeaky door hinge sounded again, and what little bit of light that had found its way to Jenna was extinguished.

"Are you all right under there?" Rebecca whispered, lifting the edge of the tarp.

Jenna sat up. "I am. You'd better go or they'll come looking for you."

"I will. What are you going to do now?"

"Is there any possibility of getting your mother alone?"

"Not until after worship."

"When is that?"

"After dinner. Everyone eats dinner at seven-thirty, and worship services start at eight and last from thirty minutes to an hour. Sometimes longer, if Elder Snow thinks we aren't pious enough."

"Hang back from the services when they're over and get your mother alone. I'll be watching for you."

"How will you stay out of sight?"

Jenna smiled and held up the bag she'd brought. "I'll be hiding in plain sight." She pulled a corner of the dress from the bag and showed it to Rebecca.

Rebecca smiled. "That was the first dress I'd ever sewn by myself."

"It's not my style, but it's lovely."

"You'll be dressed like us, but everyone knows everyone else," she said, biting her lower lip. "They'll pick you out as a stranger."

"Don't some of them wear the bonnets they sell?"

Rebecca nodded. She still looked worried. "Yes, but I don't know. It's still risky."

"I'll wait until dark to come out of hiding. Don't worry about me. Just get your mother away from the others long enough for me to talk sense into her."

"Okay." Rebecca leaned over the rim of the truck and reached for Jenna's hand. "Be careful. I never thought we'd be in danger in Sweet Salvation, but lately..." She shook her head. "I just don't know."

Jenna gripped her hand. "Don't worry. We'll get to the bottom of this."

Rebecca held the tarp higher. No one's in the barn right now. If you want to get out and find a better place to hide, now would be the time."

Jenna eased out of the back of the truck and dropped to the ground, glad she'd worn the dark shirt and jeans. "Is it dark outside?"

"It's getting dark early. There are storm clouds building from the southwest. We're supposed to get rain."

"Good. Rain will help conceal us if we need to get out tonight."

"Should I pack a bag?"

"No. If things are as sketchy as you think, you don't want to alert anyone that you're thinking of leaving."

Rebecca sighed. "It all seems so cloak-and-dagger. This place is supposed to be a sanctuary, not a terrorist training camp."

"Why would sanctuary members need training on weapons?"

"I know, I know." A door opened at the other end of the barn, allowing a dim, gray wedge of light inside. "Get down," Rebecca said.

Jenna dropped and rolled under the truck.

"What are you doing in here?" a male voice said.

"Elder Snow," Rebecca said, her voice tight. "I was loading boxes for tomorrow's market."

"You don't need to. No one will be going to market tomorrow."

"No?" she asked.

"No. We're going to spend the day in the worship hall."

"Everyone?" Rebecca squeaked.

"Everyone. So leave the boxes and get to dinner. We'll discuss the plan at worship this evening."

"Yes, Elder Snow." Rebecca hurried away.

For a long moment Jenna lay still, waiting for the man to leave the barn and close the door. He didn't. Instead, he walked around the truck and stood close enough Jenna could have reached out and touched his black shoes.

Finally, he left the barn and the door closed, plunging Jenna into darkness. Her heart raced too fast, her pulse pounding against her eardrums. Why would the elders call a commune-wide worship day out of the blue?

Jenna waited five minutes to give Elder Snow time to go back to his home and settle in to dinner. If everyone was supposed to eat at the same time, Jenna might have the opportunity to sneak into the worship hall and figure out what the elders were hiding in the basement.

She slipped out of her jeans and black shirt, pulled the dress over her head and tied it in the back, cinching the fabric in at the waist. Then she wound her hair up on her head, slipped an elastic band over it and jammed the bonnet over her head.

Jenna found her way to a side door and pushed it open a crack. Nothing moved in the compound. Though it wasn't sunset yet, the thickening clouds overhead blocked the light, giving the sky a dark and sinister dusky haze. The worship hall was the biggest building on the compound and sat dead center of the houses and other buildings, not too far from the barn.

With a quick glance left and right, Jenna slipped out of the structure and, hugging the side of the building, hurried toward the corner and the shortest distance between the two buildings.

Glancing around the corner, she didn't see anyone out and about. With a deep breath, she tipped her chin down and walked slowly across the open space between the barn and the worship hall as if she was supposed to be there, as though she were just another one of the members of the Sweet Salvation community.

No one shouted for her to stop or questioned why she was walking around at dinnertime.

When she reached the worship hall, she entered through the first door she came to, her gaze searching the interior for any movement.

Rows of chairs filled the huge room, facing a raised dais where a podium stood, draped in gold and white fabric. Nothing moved. The worship hall was empty.

Hugging the wall and keeping out of the direct light, Jenna made her way around the room, easing open any door she found, looking for the one that would take her into the basement.

One was an office with a desk, chair and bookshelves.

The next door led into a storage room with mops, buckets, brooms and folding tables stacked against the wall. As she circled the sanctuary, checking into each room, she began to think there wasn't a door leading into the basement from the inside.

At the raised dais, she stepped up, her feet connecting

with the solid wood flooring. Exposed to the room and anyone who might walk in, she hurriedly glanced around. No doors back there. Her eyes darting to the entrance, Jenna crossed the stage and stepped on a spot that didn't sound the same as the rest of the solid flooring. It had a hollowness the other planks did not.

Jenna dropped down and studied the wood. Smooth lengths of polish boards ran the length of the dais except in one spot where a square had been cut out and replaced. At one point on the square there was a small indentation a person could slip his hand into and use as a handle.

Jenna hooked her fingers beneath it and pulled. The square rose on one side, hinged on struts that locked into place when she had it at a ninety-degree angle. Leading down into the darkness was a staircase.

A trap door on the dais? Was Elder Snow expecting to have to make a quick escape?

Gathering her skirt, Jenna descended into the darkness, pulling the trap door down behind her. With the door shut all the way, not a single speck of light found its way into the basement below.

Jenna pulled her smart phone from inside her bra and switched on the flashlight app. Able to see the stairs, she continued to the bottom and shined the light around. The room was stacked with wooden crates at one end. At the other end, old tables and chairs were positioned in front of a huge chalkboard like the ones that were used back in the mid-twentieth century. Whatever had been written on the board had been erased, but not all the way.

Jenna crossed to the board and shined the light over the lines that hadn't been completely obliterated. From the residual lines, she could tell it had been a drawing of the compound with each building's position and the outer walls defined.

A chill slipped across her skin and her pulse sped. Dread filled her as she turned toward the wooden crates. Most of them were screwed shut. One at the far end of the room wasn't as securely fastened. Jenna found a crowbar leaning against the wall and pried the lid off.

The crate was filled with bolts of cloth in the ginghams and calicos typical of the dresses the women were required to wear. It didn't make sense. Why would they transport bolts of cloth in heavy wooden crates?

Unless they were hiding something underneath.

Jenna pushed the bolts aside and dug deeper, practically standing on her head to reach beneath the fabric. Her fingers touched cold hard metal. She wrapped her hand around it and dragged it from beneath the gingham. When it emerged, she gasped.

The metal belonged to the barrel of an AR 15 semi-automatic rifle, similar to the M4A1's used by the military. Familiar with the weapons from a report she'd done on the annual gun show, Jenna shivered. These weren't the regular weapons someone would use to hunt game.

Holy hell! Her hands shook as she dragged the mini-cam out of her pocket and pinned it to the front of her dress. Digging beneath the fabric in the box again, she pulled out two more AR 15s and laid them out on the floor. Further searching unearthed boxes of ammunition. Shoving the fabric to the side, she dug again and found a machine gun and belts of bullets. She laid out what she'd found, her insides quivering. If the rest of the crates contained the same, Sweet Salvation had amassed enough weapons and ammo for a small war.

Jenna pressed the mini-cam to her chest to initiate the recording and bent over the crate lid, hopefully getting all the guns and ammo in the video while she shined her smart phone flashlight over the lot. When she thought she had enough footage, she laid the weapons and ammo back in the crate and covered them with the bolts of cloth.

A door on the far end of the room swung open and lightning flashed in the sky, illuminating the loading ramp and the silhouettes of people standing outside.

Jenna killed her flashlight application and dove behind the stacks of crates filled with fabric and weapons, her heart pounding so hard she felt like it would explode out of her chest.

"Go," a gruff voice demanded.

"I'm going. You don't have push," a young female voice responded.

Jenna's heart sank when she recognized who it was.

Rebecca stepped into the basement and fumbled for the switch on the wall beside the door. Light flooded the room.

Jenna shrank further into the shadows behind the crates. Peering through a gap between them, she could see the two women and the man following them. Jenna had seen him in the news recently talking about all the good Sweet Salvation was doing for the community.

Huh!

"Don't hurt my daughter. Please." Lissa, Rebecca's mother pleaded. "She didn't hurt anyone."

"She had contraband," the man said. "Cell phones are the work of the devil and not allowed on the compound."

"So, take it," Lissa said, following Rebecca into the room. "You don't have to lock us in the basement. We know it was wrong and promise not to do it again."

"I'm not promising anything," Rebecca said. "I want out of this compound, and Mom, you're coming with me."

"Neither one of you is going anywhere until Elder Snow says so." The man stepped in behind them and closed the door, twisting a key in the lock.

Jenna hunkered over her cell phone to block the light it generated, and synced the mini-camcorder's data to her phone. Once synchronization was complete, she drafted a text to Toby.

Trouble in paradise. See video. Trapped in basement of worship hall with contraband.

Attaching the video to the text, she hit SEND. With only two bars of reception, the video would be painfully slow transferring, but it had to go. The outside world had to know what was going on inside the walls of the Sweet Salvation community.

"What are you looking for?" Rebecca asked, her voice jerking Jenna back to her dilemma. The man who'd entered the basement with the women had crossed to the crates behind which Jenna hid.

Jenna pressed the smart phone to her belly, hoping to hide the screen light while the text message took its time sending.

The man squatted out of Jenna's visual range. "Someone has been down here," he straightened with the crate lid in his hands.

Jenna cringed. She'd returned the items to the box, but forgotten to replace the lid.

The man laid the lid over the crate and pressed his finger to his ear. "Elder Snow, we may have a problem."

The man had a radio headset. For a compound set up to operate on only the basics, they were far too well-equipped with military-like hardware.

He turned toward Rebecca. "Did you enter this room without permission?"

Rebecca shook her head. "How could I? The other women barely let me out of their sights."

"You managed to hide a cell phone on your person without them finding it."

"But they did," Rebecca pointed out. "We're here now, aren't we?"

The lock on the door twisted and the door opened. Elder Snow entered, a heavy frown marring his forehead.

"What is the meaning of this? Why are these women here?"

"Miss Rebecca had a cell phone on her, and I believe they broke into this room and tampered with our supplies."

Elder Snow's brows dipped even further. He walked up to Lissa. "Is this your doing?"

Lissa shook her head, her eyes rounding. "My daughter doesn't understand the evil of cell phones. She knows now. Let us leave, and you'll have no more trouble with us again."

Rebecca slipped an arm around her mother. "I know about the rules. But I also know that you're hiding something."

Elder Snow stepped up to Rebecca and slapped her hard on the cheek, knocking her to the ground. "You know nothing."

Jenna rose halfway to her feet, ready to launch herself at the man hitting her cousin.

The one who'd escorted them into the basement cleared his throat. "They might know more than we want them to." He turned toward the boxes where Jenna hid.

Jenna eased back to the ground.

The man touched the crate Jenna had rummaged through. "This lid was on the floor. I know I replaced it the last time we were in here. Someone was looking inside."

"You and I are the only ones allowed in this room," Elder Snow said.

"What's in it?" Rebecca asked, pressing her hand to her split lip as she rose to her feet. "Guns? I heard the men shooting this morning. This is supposed to be a peaceful community, free of drugs and violence."

Elder Snow swung his big arm, backhanding her.

Rebecca flew across the floor, sprawling across the ground.

"Don't," her mother cried out and flung herself over her daughter's body.

"Shut up. Both of you," Elder Snow shouted. "We are a peaceful community, living a simple and pure life."

Rebecca eased her mother aside and sat up, wiping blood from her mouth. "Then why the guns?"

Elder Snow's eyes narrowed. "We protect what's ours from those who might try to take it away from us." He stepped toward Rebecca, drawing his arm back as if to strike her again.

"Stop!" Jenna rose from her position. She couldn't let this man hit the girl again. "Stop hitting her."

The man near the crates jumped back, startled by Jenna's sudden appearance.

Taking advantage of his temporary withdrawal, Jenna rounded the other side of the crates and threw herself in front of Elder Snow. "You have no right to hit this woman."

Before she could duck, his hand snaked out, slapping her hard in the face. Her head snapped back and pain shot through her cheek.

"You are an intruder and have no right to tell me what to do. I could have you shot for trespassing."

Jenna refused to touch her throbbing cheek. Instead, she flung back her shoulders and dared him to hit her again. "Will you have me shot with one of the military weapons you've been hiding in these crates? You know some of those weapons are illegal, and yet you brought them into your so-called peaceful community among the women and children."

Elder Snow's cheeks turned a ruddy red. "You have no idea what you're talking about. We've built a model community full of loyal citizens who would do anything for the good of Sweet Salvation."

"Even kill people? Are you willing to sacrifice innocent children?"

His nostrils flared and he lifted his chin. "If the lord wills it."

"You mean if you will it." Jenna faced off with the man.

"Elder Mathis, take these women into the adjustment room," the older man said. "Our people are waiting for us above."

Mathis stepped forward and reached for Rebecca.

Jenna launched herself at the man, knocking him to the side. "Leave her alone!"

Lissa rose to her feet, crying and wringing her hands. "Please. Don't hurt my daughter."

Before Jenna could straighten, she heard Rebecca scream.

Elder Snow had her by the hair, pulling back hard, exposing her neck where he held a wickedly sharp knife to her throat. "Back off or I'll kill her."

Lissa crumpled to the floor sobbing. "This is not right. You can't hurt my little girl."

"He's going to hurt a lot of little girls if he does what I think he's planning," Jenna stared at the crazy leader of the commune, knowing by the way he spoke and the remorseless look in his eyes, he meant what he'd said. He'd kill Rebecca. Jenna straightened. "Let Rebecca go. I'll go along with you peacefully."

Mathis grabbed her arm and yanked it up behind her back.

Pain knifed through her shoulder as he shoved her toward a door on the other side of the crates.

Behind her, Elder Snow said, "You. Go with her."

"Please, please, don't hurt my daughter," Lissa wailed, her sobs following Jenna's progression toward the dark doorway.

Mathis yanked the door open and pushed Jenna down a long hallway with doors on both sides and locks on the outside. When he reached the last door at the end, he twisted the lock, jerked the door open and shoved her in. He didn't stop until he had her pinned to the wall, smashing her face against cool concrete blocks. He kicked her feet to a wide stance and finally released his hold on her arm.

Jenna nearly cried in relief.

Mathis ran his hands over her body, stopping when

he reached the pocket at her waist where she'd tucked the cell phone after she'd sent her text.

"Elder Snow. You should see this." Mathis held up the phone and hit the on button. The screen flashed to life, displaying the text message she'd sent and the video attachment.

Elder Snow shoved Rebecca and her mother into the room, snatched at the cell phone and muttered curses no preacher should ever say. "Join the congregation in the worship hall and lock the doors. Tell the men we're going to code Rapture."

Mathis's face blanched and he stammered, "Yes, Elder Snow."

Jenna's blood ran cold at the look on Snow's face. "What do you mean by code Rapture?"

The two men backed out of the room.

Elder Snow shook his head. "You have no idea what you've done. You will, soon enough. But by then, it will be too late for you and the good people of Sweet Salvation." Then he closed the door and the click of the deadbolt lock echoed in the complete darkness.

"What did he mean by that?" Rebecca said. "Too late for the people of Sweet Salvation?"

"The Rapture is when God will reclaim the true believers, and they will ascend into Heaven," Lissa's voice sounded like a chant from rote memory or the echo of a pastor's preaching.

"Does he intend for all the members of Sweet Salvation to die?" Jenna asked, the chill of the cool basement permeating her skin all the way to her bones. "Does he intend to kill them?"

"He will expect them to give their lives unto the Lord," Lissa whispered.

"All of them?" Jenna asked. "What about the children?"

"God will welcome them, too," Rebecca's mother said, her tone eerily calm, as though she was reciting something she'd said often.

"And they will do this?"

"Yes," Lissa said.

"Elder Snow is insane." Determined to find a way out and warn the congregation, Jenna felt her way along the wall until concrete gave way to the cool metal door. She ran her hands over the smooth metal. There was no knob on their side.

"There's no way out," Jenna said.

Lissa sobbed.

Rebecca bumped into Jenna, her hands out in front of her. "Now what do we do?" she asked.

Jenna sank to the cool floor and buried her face in her hands. "We pray the cavalry arrives in time to save us."

10

———

Dustin's brothers didn't question his request, they dove into the SUV with Toby.

"Shouldn't we take weapons?"

"That compound is full of women and children. We have to get in and neutralize the threat before we call in the sheriff's department or the ATF. Otherwise it'll be another massacre like what happened at the Mount Carmel Center when David Koresh clashed with the ATF over illegal firearms and explosives."

Toby, from his position in the back seat, leaned forward. "If the leader of this group is even half as crazy as Koresh, it could be another blood bath with innocents being hurt or killed."

"Exactly," Dustin said. "The video Toby forwarded from Jenna indicates they have enough arms and ammo to start a war, and they've trapped Jenna inside the compound. Once bullets start flying, innocent people will be hurt. We have to go in unarmed and take out their leader with minimal use of force." Even though he wanted to kill the man for trapping Jenna in the compound.

He fought to control the panic rising inside. It was just another mission, like so many he'd been on before. Except he wouldn't have his modified M4A1 rifle or his nine-millimeter handgun. He did have a knife and wouldn't hesitate to use it if it meant saving Jenna's life.

"I don't like going in without my own weapons," Houston said.

"You and me both," Adam agreed. "At least I was able to score the bulletproof vests and night vision goggles. They just need to be back in the armory by morning."

Dustin's jaw tightened. "They will be."

Adam shook his head. "You say that like this'll be a slam-dunk. None of us have had the advantage of being inside the compound to know what we'll be up against."

"Thanks to Toby, he was able to pull a satellite photo off the Internet," Dustin said.

"Glad I could be of help." Toby leaned back. "I'm sorry I didn't stop Jenna from going in the first place."

"At least you had the good sense to tag her with a tracking device."

Adam held the tracker. Toby had given the men a crash-course in how to use it.

A mile away from the road leading into the compound, Dustin slowed the SUV, turned off the lights and drove in blackout conditions until they were only a half-mile away. Then he pulled off the road, driving the SUV between two scrub cedars, effectively hiding the vehicle from view.

All four men climbed out into the darkness with only the city lights of Waco reflecting off the low-hanging clouds. It started misting lightly as they stood in front of the vehicle checking their gear and tightening the buckles on the bulletproof vests. Adam handed the GPS tracker to Dustin. "You'll want this to find your girl."

Dustin clutched the device in his hand, thankful Toby had the foresight to equip Jenna with the tag that would help them find her.

"Toby," Dustin said. "You're to stay here and guard the vehicle."

"I'm going in with you," the younger man argued. "It's my fault Jenna's in there to begin with."

Dustin snorted. "Do you really think you could have talked her out of it?"

Toby grinned. "No." His smile faded. "But I should have tried harder."

"She'd have gone anyway," Dustin said. "She has family in there." Though she'd dumped him after only two days of being engaged, the woman loved her family and would do anything for them. Even the nutty ones.

"When we've been gone for one hour, you know what to do, right?" Dustin asked.

With a nod, Toby recited his job. "I'll forward the text with the video to Adam's friend on the SWAT team and my buddy in the sheriff's department, following up with a telephone call to get them out there ASAP."

"Hopefully, they won't come in guns 'blazin'," Houston said.

Dustin's fists tightened. "We're going to sever the snake's head and stop this uprising before it gets going."

Toby's eyes widened. "You're going to cut off the elder's head?"

Houston laughed. "No, but we're going to take him out of the equation so the rest of his following won't have their leader." He handed out rolls of duct tape. "We'll use this as our best weapon."

"Duct tape."

Dustin nodded. "That's right. Immobilize them without killing them. We're not in the Middle East with the U.S. government backing us up. We're on American soil. Our own people won't understand if we go in slitting the throats of what appear to be innocent, peaceful folk."

"The idea is to do this on the down-low," Adam said. "Take out the leader and hold him until the authorities can sort through the truth."

"In many terrorist organizations, if you take away their leader, they fall apart," Dustin explained.

"The people of Sweet Salvation have been peaceful for the most part," Adam reminded them. "Let's not hurt any more than we have to. It would be even better if we could get in and out without being discovered. I don't want any of us up on charges of breaking and entering or false imprisonment when we catch the leader."

"The problem is that we don't know what line of bull-shit their leader has been feeding them or how wide-spread it is," Houston pointed out. "If he's brainwashed all the adults, we may be up against a lot more opposition than we're prepared for."

"Well, we're not inside yet, and we won't get there if we don't get moving." Dustin headed into the brush.

Houston followed, and Adam brought up the rear.

Moving quickly, they arrived at the seven-foot tall, concrete block wall surrounding the compound. The gate was another quarter of a mile to the north. A single guard walked along the outside of the fence near the entrance, holding an old-fashioned lantern in front of him. From the distance, Dustin could see that he carried a gun of some sort slung over his shoulder. When the man turned away from them, Dustin pointed to the fence.

Houston reached it first, bent and cupped his hands.

Dustin stepped into his hands and scaled the wall. He laid flat on the concrete bricks, slipped the night vision goggles in place and checked the other side, looking for the ghostly green images of warm bodies moving about. When he didn't see any, he whispered. "Clear."

Adam stepped in Houston's hands and pulled himself up to the top. Then the two brothers straddled the fence, leaned down and grabbed Houston's hands, hauling him up between them.

All three men dropped to the other side before the guard turned and headed back their way.

Once on the ground, they sprinted toward the nearest

building. Dustin had his NVGs in place. Houses lined the outer edges of the community along with several barns. A large building took up the center of the compound. Toby had identified it as the worship hall from old news reports. No green images appeared in his NVGs. No one was moving about.

Jenna's text said she was trapped in the basement of the worship hall. Dustin's instinct was to barge in, kick ass and find his woman. But to do this right, he had to keep calm and execute this mission with clean, cool precision in order to find the leader and head off a disaster with the potential to hurt a lot of people, including Jenna. If she was truly trapped in the basement and the leader decided to burn the place down, she'd die before they could get in, find her and get her out.

His belly clenched. This was not exactly the scenario he had in mind for declaring his love for the woman who'd never been a day off his mind. He'd rather have met her at her house, taken her into his arms and whispered his love in her ear. In Dustin's version, Jenna would have flung her arms around his neck and declared she loved him, too. He'd ask her to marry him, she'd say yes and they'd consummate their engagement in some mind-blowing sex for the duration of his visit to Waco.

Instead, he and his brothers were staging an assault on a commune.

Dustin waved Houston to the right while he and Adam circled around the other side of the sprawling worship center. The sound of someone preaching murmured through the walls.

The backside of the structure was two stories, unlike the front's single story, indicating a half-buried basement below. Jenna had to be there. Dustin hugged the shadows of the building opposite the worship hall and bent over the GPS tracker, double-checking Jenna's location before he forced his way through the door. The indicator pointed to that building. A loading dock took up half of the exterior wall with a wide overhead door and a narrower single door beside it.

"She's in there," he whispered to Adam.

Adam nodded. "Let's do this."

They would get in and free Jenna. Then they'd go after the community leader, separate him from the others and remove him from the premises until which time the local authorities or the ATF could get there and take over.

Dustin started forward.

Adam slammed an arm against his chest, stopping him.

The back door to the worship hall opened and men poured out, all carrying weapons.

"Damn," Adam muttered and sank back behind a stand of bushes.

They waited until the line of men scattered outward, heading for the outer perimeter.

Dustin hoped Houston had found a good position to lay low and stay out of sight of the commune's troops. The men barely knew how to carry the weapons. How well could they shoot? The drizzle they'd started out with grew heavier, turning into a light rain, making it harder to see and to be seen. Hopefully, the men of the commune would assume the people inside the compound walls were the good guys, giving Dustin, Adam and Houston a shot at getting to the building. Once inside, if there were others still being assigned weapons, the brothers might run into trouble.

Dustin nodded to Adam. "Ready?"

Adam answered by hurrying across the opening between the two buildings. When he reached the outside wall of the worship hall, he waited for Dustin to join him. They converged on the back door where Houston joined them.

"Anything happening out front?" Dustin asked, softly.

Houston shook his head. "Outside doors are locked. Sounds like a sermon going on inside."

"Cover us." Dustin told him. "We're going in."

"I got your back." Houston hunkered down in a shadow near the base of the loading dock.

Dustin and Adam climbed the steps and tried the single door. It swung inward into a large room filled with open wooden crates. Four men remained in the room, two of which were digging through a crate. The other two were loading ammunition into a banana clip. All four looked up as Dustin entered the room. Adam followed, twisting the deadbolt lock behind him.

Dustin lifted his NVGs and nodded. "Gentlemen, I suggest you put down your weapons."

The two men loading the clips leaped to their feet, grabbed AR 15s and would have shoved the banana clips into the chamber, but Adam and Dustin reached them before they made the connection.

The Sweet Salvation men might have been trained to fire their weapons, but they were not skilled in hand-to-hand combat and went down easily. Adam quickly wrapped duct tape around his guy's wrists, securing them behind the man's back and then handed the tape to Dustin who did the same in record time.

The other two men who'd been digging in the crates yanked out AR 15s and pointed them at Dustin and Adam.

"Let them go, or we'll shoot," said a man dressed in simple black trousers and a homespun white shirt, his voice quavering.

Dustin nodded at the weapons pointed at him and Adam as he completed a circle of tape around his captive's wrists. "We aren't here to hurt anyone. We're trying to stop your people from being harmed. Put down the gun."

The one closest to them shook his head. "No. You need to leave. Now. Or I'll sh-shoot."

Dustin strode across the floor toward the man closest to him. "You don't want to kill anyone."

"I will martyr myself in the name of God." The man squeezed the trigger. Nothing happened.

His lips quirking, Dustin jerked the rifle out of the man's hands. "The weapon is only dangerous when it's loaded." He threw the rifle aside, grabbed the man's arm and twisted, spinning him around. In seconds, he had the man's wrists bound and a piece of tape over his mouth. Adam handled the other man, leading him to a corner of the room.

Once all four men were secured in duct tape, Dustin glanced around the large room filled with crates. Several doors led off the main warehouse room. If the basement was as large as the building above, the warehouse storage where they were standing was only half of the space available beneath the worship hall.

Dustin pointed to a door. "Adam, take that one. I've got the middle."

When Dustin opened the middle doorway, he discovered a long hallway, leading down the center of the building. As he walked down the hall, he checked inside each of the rooms lining the corridor, his stomach turning over as he realized each door had a deadbolt lock on the outside. He could hear the sound of someone preaching coming from somewhere above him and very near. The echo of people chanting followed every pause from the speaker. Adam entered the hallway behind him.

"Nothing inside these rooms," Adam said, his voice low and soft.

The doors Dustin opened were each thick and seemed to be solid, the rooms on the other side were more like individual cells. Dustin didn't call out for Jenna, afraid his voice would carry to whoever was preaching above him. He had to find her and get her out before the congregation adjourned or the armed men returned and found their comrades trussed up like pigs for the slaughter.

About the time Dustin smelled the rotten-egg scent of gas, Adam spoke, "I smell gas. Either there's a leak, or someone has bigger plans for the worship hall and everyone in it."

"Get out," Dustin said. "I'll find Jenna and bring her out on my own. Get out," he insisted.

"I'm not leaving without you."

Dustin ran to the next door and flung it open. Only four more to check. God, he hoped he found her before the whole building went up.

Adam jerked the door open on the other side of the hallway. Dustin opened the next and then the last door at the end of the long hallway, beside a wooden ladder leading up to the ceiling. The lock on this door was engaged. He flipped it and opened the door. Three women scrambled out into the hall, all talking at once.

When he untangled the lot, he found Jenna and pulled her into his arms.

"Thank God you came when you did." Jenna clung to him and kissed his lips. Then she leaned back. "We have to get out of here. I think Elder Snow is going to euthanize his congregation."

"We can't leave all those people to die."

The smell of smoke filtered in from above their heads.

"Oh, god, he's really going through with it. He'd going to burn the worship hall down with everyone inside."

"Not everyone. The men got out with weapons and ammunition."

"That leaves the women and children," Jenna's voice choked. "Snow is going to martyr them by burning the worship hall."

Shouts above them grew louder and screams could be heard, rising into a roaring crescendo.

"He told his assistant to lock the doors. Those people are trapped inside. They'll die."

The sound of a door opening overhead alerted Dustin. A square of light pierced the dim lighting of the long hallway and smoke poured into the opening above. Screams and cries filled the air as panic ensued.

"Hide," Jenna whispered. "Someone's coming down from the sanctuary."

Dustin held Jenna's hand and slipped into the nearest doorway. Adam and Houston gathered the two women and hid in the cell on the other side.

They waited while a man eased down the ladder, pulling the trap door closed over his head, shutting off the spread of smoke and muffling the screams of women and children.

When the man reached the bottom, he turned and hurried toward the other end of the hallway.

"That's Elder Snow. The bastard is leaving his people to die in the worship hall." Jenna surged forward.

Dustin stopped her. "Let us take care of him." He slipped past her.

Adam and Houston burst into the hallway at the same time and they jumped Elder Snow.

"What is the meaning of this?" the older man insisted, trying to pull his arms free of the Ford men's grip. He glanced up at the trap door. Smoke sifted through the cracks between the planks, burning Dustin's lungs. He gave the preacher a rough shake. "Did you set the place on fire?"

"Our people will not be governed by others. They have the right to live the way the want or die for what they believe in."

"They have the right to live or die, but their children do not deserve to die for what their parents have been brainwashed into believing by a crazy man." Dustin shook his head. "Hell, we don't have time to deal with you." He slammed his elbow into the man's face, broke his nose and sent him flying backward to land on his ass. "You had no right to sentence those women and children to death."

"And you left them," Lissa stood over Elder Snow, her brows puckered in accusation. "You left good people to die."

"We can't let that happen," Rebecca said. She ran for the ladder and hurried up to the sanctuary above, pushing the trap door open.

The screaming grew louder.

"It's too late." Elder Snow sat up, blood dripping from his nose. "Let them go to their god. Let them martyr themselves in His name."

"We're not going to let them die on our watch." Dustin pulled out his roll of duct tape, secured the elder's wrists together behind him and slapped some over his mouth, tired of listening to his crazy talk and desperate to help save the people in the worship hall.

Jenna left his side and raced to the ladder, following Rebecca up into the sanctuary.

"Jenna!" Dustin cried out. "Don't go up there. We'll open the doors from the outside."

She didn't hear him over the shouts and screams.

"Go after her," Adam said. "We'll handle it from the outside. We'll get those people out."

Dustin didn't argue. He started up the ladder and into the murky, smoky room above. Jenna and Rebecca stood on a dais shouting into the panicked crowd. "Come up onto the dais. There's a way out through here."

Dustin climbed up the rest of the way and stood beside Jenna. Then he raised his voice above the cacophony of noise and called out in a calming voice, "Please, everyone stay calm and get down on your knees. The lower you are, the less smoke you'll inhale."

To prove it, he dropped to his haunches and pulled Jenna down beside him.

11

Jenna coughed, the smoke burning her lungs. She waved toward a woman and her two small children. "Please, save your children."

The woman coughed and yanked her children away from Jenna's outstretched hand. "You are the devil risen up from the fires of hell!"

"Lady, if I'm the devil, where did your leader go? Elder Snow snuck out the back and left you and all the women and children trapped in here to die."

"We're going to our Lord. He will grant us Sweet Salvation," she said, while her baby cried.

"Let him grant it to you. But don't condemn your children to death." Dustin leaped down off the dais, grabbed the baby from her arms and handed her to Jenna. "Get her out." He took the little boy from her and climbed back on the stage. "If you want to see your children again in this life, you'll come with me."

Rebecca jumped off the stage and did the same, taking a child from a mother's arms and hurried back up onto the stage.

Jenna stood at the trap door, clueless and more desperate to get out as the smoke thickened. She was strong, but she wasn't sure she could manage carrying a baby down the ladder.

Dustin set his charge on the platform beside her. "Hold onto him. Don't let go." Then he was down the ladder and reached up. "Lower the baby to me," he called from below.

"No, that's my baby. Those are my children!" The woman leaped onto the stage. Before she reached her, Jenna lowered the baby to Dustin. "You want your baby, lady, go get her."

Dustin set the baby on the ground and reached up for the boy.

Jenna dragged the little guy to the opening. He kicked and screamed, crying for his mother. He landed a few good blows to Jenna's shins before she had him dangling over the trap door and lowered him to Dustin.

Jenna turned to the woman. "It's your choice to live or die, but don't let a fanatic kill your children."

The woman shook her head. "We were supposed to go to the Lord."

"And Elder Snow was chosen to send you? He's a liar, and if he succeeds, he'll be a murderer of women and children. He's not God's messenger. Please, go with your children. They're crying for their mother. You know you love them."

Tears filled the woman's eyes. "I do love my babies."

"Then go." Jenna led the woman to the ladder and watched as she descended into the basement.

Rebecca appeared beside her carrying a baby, followed by a woman with two other children. "These people want to live."

The woman handed her children down to Dustin and lowered herself to the ground.

Lissa appeared beside Jenna. "Let me help."

Jenna pointed to the basement. "Take over from Dustin. He can be of more help up here getting everyone else out."

She nodded and hurried down the ladder.

Dustin climbed up and gathered Jenna in his arms. "Get out now. The smoke's getting bad."

"I can't leave these babies to die," she said, her eyes tearing from the smoke, her heart swelling with her love for this man who'd rescued her from certain death and now worked to save others. "Let's get them out." She ripped a long strip of fabric from the hem of her dress and handed it to him, then ripped another for herself. They tied it around their noses and mouths and went to work saving the people of Sweet Salvation.

One by one, they hustled women and their children to the dais and down through the trap door. Soon a fire brigade of women lined the hallway in the basement, hurrying children out into the open.

But it wasn't fast enough, and the smoke was so thick Jenna worried she and Dustin wouldn't get out before they were overcome. With fifty or more women and children still in the sanctuary, they wouldn't be able to save them all.

Jenna coughed and hacked, her eyes streaming as she helped another woman up on the dais.

"Go. I'll get the rest.

"You can't," she coughed. "There are too many."

By now, the remainder of the women crowded around them, crying and shoving their children forward.

"You have to leave," Dustin told Jenna. "I don't want you to die. I love you." He held her for a moment and then pushed her toward the trap door.

Her heart burned with her love for this man at the same time her lungs burned with the smoke filling them. "I won't leave without you. And in case we don't make it out alive, I love you. I've always loved you."

At that moment, the fire burned through one of the walls and it cracked, falling several feet before it stopped. Roof timbers creaked, and the remaining women dropped to the floor, covering their children with their bodies.

"Please, go, Jenna," Dustin begged.

She shook her head and quietly handed another child down into the basement, refusing to leave until all the children were saved. If she left one behind, she couldn't live with herself.

With the roof threatening to fall on top of all of them

and too many people to get out before it did, Jenna looked across at Dustin. The man was black with smoke and soot. But he was the most beautiful man inside and out and she loved him with all her heart.

One more child. Two. By then she moved like an automaton, lifting and lowering children until her arms ached. Dustin, by her side, did the same. It was only a matter of time before the fire claimed them. She would die beside the only man she ever loved.

A crash filled the air at the far end near the locked entrance to the sanctuary. The wall caved inward and lights shined through the dense smoke.

Women and children screamed and flocked toward Jenna and Dustin, nearly toppling them into the open trap door.

The lights backed away from the door and smoke poured out of the building, and then the lights raced forward again and another crash shook the walls and floor.

"Someone's driving a vehicle into the wall." Dustin waded through the crowd of women and children, ducked low and ran through the sanctuary toward the crash site and was quickly engulfed in the black smoke.

"Dustin!" Jenna cried out.

The sound of sirens pierced the chaos inside the worship hall. Soon men appeared like ghosts in the smoke and hurried toward the remaining victims. They gathered children in their arms and led the women back through the smoke.

Jenna continued to help some down the ladder while others were taken out the front. When she helped the last woman down the ladder, she collapsed, exhausted and too tired to move. With the huge hole in the side of the building, some of the smoke cleared, but the fire licked at the walls and up to the roof. A loud snap above her made her turn in time to see the beam running down the middle of the sanctuary crack. The ceiling buckled, swayed and then came crashing down. Jenna rolled over the open trap door just in time, falling the nine feet to the hard floor below. When she hit, what little light from the fire above was extinguished, and she welcomed oblivion.

Dustin had just pushed the last woman and her small children into the arms of a sheriff's deputy and turned back to the sanctuary when the roof collapsed, sending a blast of smoke, soot and flames out the sides. He dropped to the ground, covered his head and waited until the smoke and heat dissipated, then he leaped to his feet to survey the disaster, his heartbeat grinding to a stop.

Jenna.

Dear God, Jenna was still in there. He started for the building but Adam and Houston caught him before he ran into the raging fire.

Rain beat down on him washing soot into his eyes. If tears mixed in with the rain, he couldn't tell, nor did he care. He'd left Jenna inside the building.

He fought against his brothers' hold on his arms. "Let me go. Jenna's still in there."

"If she was still inside the worship hall when it fell, it

would do absolutely no good for you to try to get to her from up here." Adam held on onto his arm, refusing to release him. "Anything beneath that roof would have been crushed."

"But I left her inside."

"Maybe she got out through the basement before the roof fell," Houston offered.

"Dustin, Adam, Houston," Toby leaped out of a sheriff's vehicle that had just arrived in front of the destroyed sanctuary. "You don't know how glad I am to see you guys." He stared around at the women and children huddled in clusters, covered in soot and ashes, sobbing. "What happened here? Where's Jenna?"

Dustin shook free of his brothers' hold and ran toward the rear of the building to the basement loading dock. The roof remained intact and people ran out of the open overhead door. The men, who'd exited with guns earlier, had returned to help, throwing their weapons on the ground.

Steady rain fell over the people of Sweet Salvation as families searched for their loved ones. A little girl stood, drenched in her dress, wailing, tears mingling with the rain. A woman ran to her, scooped her up in her arms and hugged her tight.

With a flashlight in his hand, Dustin shined it at the people he passed, searching the faces, praying he'd find Jenna among them. He ran from one cluster to another without locating her. He finally reached the loading dock and climbed the stairs, entering through the overhead door. The men he and his brothers had bound with duct tape had been released, presumably by the women they were helping to herd the last of children out of the sanctuary. Still, no Jenna.

"The hallway in the back," Adam said, entering the basement behind Dustin. Houston was close behind.

Dustin shined his light down the hallway. Nothing moved, but there were several lumps on the floor. His lungs burned and his heart ached as he bent to study the first lump he came to. It turned out to be a child's blanket and rag doll. Relief was short-lived when his flashlight beam encountered another. A woman's bag filled with books and diapers lay scattered against the wall. Smoke filtered in from the collapsed roof above as he neared the dark end of the hallway and the final pile of rags on the floor. He dropped to his knees and cried as he felt for a pulse. Several seconds passed before the reassuring thump of blood pushing through her veins nudged his fingertips.

"He found her," Adam said. "Dustin, do you need help?"

He managed to croak an answer past the lump in his throat. "No." He scooped her up in his arms and stood. "Get Snow out of the room behind you, Adam."

Adam and Houston opened the door and dragged Elder Snow to his feet.

Dustin didn't wait to see that he was okay, he was more concerned about Jenna and why she wasn't waking up.

He didn't stop until he carried her out into the rain and several yards away from the burning building. "Jenna, darlin'. Please wake up," he said, holding her close to his chest.

Adam, Houston and Toby joined him.

"How's Jenna?" Toby asked.

"I don't know. She hasn't woken up."

"Her forehead's bleeding." Houston pointed to her temple.

Her wound had torn open and blood oozed out, mixed with rain, and made a dark trail down the side of her face.

"Toby!" Two women ran up to the younger man. "Have you seen Jenna?" the younger one asked then spied Dustin. "Oh dear Lord." She clapped a hand to her mouth and tears streamed down her face. "Is she...?"

Dustin shook his head. "She's alive, but we need to get her to a hospital."

The woman in his arms stirred, and her eyes blinked open. "No hospital," she said, her voice rasping.

"Jenna?" Dustin nearly laughed with relief.

She wrapped her arms around his neck and pressed her lips to his. "Thank God you got out alive."

"Me?" He kissed her. "You were the one I was worried about. When the roof caved in, I lost ten years off my life."

"I saw it coming and rolled into the trap door." She gently touched her temple where the wound was open and bleeding, and winced. "But I'm okay." She smiled at him. Her white teeth shone in her grimy face.

Dustin couldn't remember a time when she was more beautiful than at that moment. He kissed her again. "You're going to a hospital. You were unconscious. You could have a concussion."

"I have a headache and my lungs burn, but I'll live and it's raining. God, it feels good. And I'm in the arms of the only man I've ever loved. What more could I ask for?"

"I plan on you being in my arms a whole lot more. So don't argue with me when I tell you that you're going to see a doctor." He strode toward the blinking lights of an ambulance.

It appeared as though all of the county emergency services and half of the Waco fire department had arrived at the Sweet Salvation compound, along with every sheriff's deputy and a contingent of ATF personnel.

Dustin wasn't stopping to answer questions, nor was he waiting in line to have Jenna seen by the medical staff on site. He barged through the gaggle of women and children. "My fiancé needs assistance now."

An EMT appeared beside him and pointed to the ambulance. "Let's get her out of the rain and check her out."

"I'm fine," she said. "Put me down. I'll show you."

"Ma'am, smoke inhalation is nothing to play around with." The EMT shined a light in her eyes. "Neither is concussion. Please, let us take care of you."

The emergency medical technicians pulled the

gurney out of the back of the ambulance. Dustin laid Jenna on the mattress and stepped back allowing the medical personnel access to check her over.

They attached an oxygen mask to her face, checked her vitals and loaded her into the ambulance.

"I'm going with her."

"Sir, it would be better if you followed behind."

Jenna pulled the mask off her face. "He's coming with me, or I'm going with him."

"Okay, okay." The technician grinned. "The woman has a mind of her own, doesn't she?"

Dustin laughed and climbed in beside the technician. "You have no idea."

The back door closed and the ambulance pulled away from the remains of the Sweet Salvation sanctuary.

Dustin held Jenna's hand while the EMT established an IV. "Before another disaster happens and another minute goes by, I want you to know..." He took a breath and squeezed her hand. "I love you Jenna Turner. More now than ever. I lead an insane and dangerous life, although sometimes I think you live one even more dangerous than mine. The point is, I can't always be there for you, but when I am, I'll love you enough to make up for all the time I'm away. Would you consider marrying me and coming to live with me in Virginia? I promise to love you until the day I die, like I've loved you from the first time I kissed you in the sixth grade."

Tears pooled in Jenna's eyes, and she pulled the mask off her face. "Dustin Ford, I thought you'd never come to your senses and return to me. I never stopped loving you for a minute."

He frowned. "Then why did you break our engagement?"

"I knew you wouldn't pursue your dream of being a Navy SEAL if you married me. You dreamed of joining the Navy since you were a little kid. I didn't want to be the one thing standing in the way of your dream." The tears slid down her cheeks. "And you did it. I was so proud. But then you didn't come back for me."

"I thought you hated me." He lifted her hand to his lips and kissed it, soot and all. "You broke my heart into a million pieces when you told me to go away. I couldn't see you again without wanting to reach out and hold you in my arms."

She smiled through her tears. "I'd have been there in a heartbeat."

"Call me a coward, but I couldn't take the rejection again, if you didn't love me as much as I loved you." He brushed the hair back from her forehead. "I can't believe I'm sitting here with you and you love me." Dustin shook his head.

"Believe it, buster."

"So, what's it to be?" He held her hand, his gaze connecting with hers. "Will you marry me?"

"Always planned on it. I still have the ring you gave me." She pulled the necklace out of the collar of her dress, and the simple diamond ring dangled from it. "I never gave up hope we'd be together one day."

He dropped to the floor of the ambulance and gathered her in his arms. "I love you, Jenna, and I never want to be without you again." As Dustin lowered his mouth to hers, the vehicle slowed to a stop.

The EMT cleared his throat, reminding them that they had an audience. "We're at the hospital. This reunion is very touching, but we need to get you inside and get back to the compound for the next patient."

"Of course." Jenna raised a finger. "But just one more minute. I want that kiss."

She wrapped her arms around Dustin's neck and sealed the deal with a kiss he wouldn't soon forget. Not that he'd ever forgotten this incredibly brave, crazy, beautiful woman. Now she would be his forever.

SEAL'S DEFIANCE

TAKE NO PRISONERS BOOK #7

New York Times & *USA Today*
Bestselling Author

ELLE JAMES

SEALS
DEFIANCE

New York Times & USA Today Bestselling Author
ELLE JAMES

CHAPTER 1

"It's fucking Grand Central Station in Samada tonight," Declan O'Shea muttered into his radio. On point for this mission, he studied the small village in semi-arid, southwestern Somalia. Either Intel had it wrong or the al-Shabaab leader, Emir Fuad Hassan Umar, had called a meeting of all his leaders, or he had beefed up his security in the past twenty-four hours.

"I count fifteen bogeys on the south corner." Swede had moved into position on the southern end of the village.

"Same on the north," Fish reported. "Tight perimeter as well. No one sleeping, yet."

"Over twenty stationed outside our target structure," Irish said from his location thirty yards from one of the grass huts on the east end of the village. He hugged the shadows, his night vision goggles pushed up on his helmet, unnecessary with the full moon lighting the sky like daytime. Not conducive to a surprise attack on the emir.

Orders were orders. Over two hours ago, the eighteen-man team had fast-roped from the two Black Hawk helicopters several miles from the target. They'd moved in on foot, carrying the explosives and weapons they needed.

SEAL Team 10 had been tasked to decapitate the head of a growing al-Shabaab faction led by a murderous former member of the Somali Islamic Courts Union who'd wiped out entire villages of people. In one village, he and his men had gone through, hut by hut, and killed the men, raped the women and slaughtered the children. When they were through pillaging, they burned the structures to the ground. In other villages, he'd wiped out the entire population and strewn their corpses for the scavenger birds.

A freelance news reporter happened upon the scene shortly after. The pictures he'd sent back to be printed in the US and the UK newspapers had shocked the western-ers. But not until the rebels raided a small women's college in a suburb of Mogadishu, kidnapped all the females and sold them into slavery, did the U.S. adminis-tration take action.

Langley did their magic with satellite images, and SEAL Team 10 got the alert to stand ready to deploy.

They hadn't known their destination until they boarded the C-130 aircraft bound for a joint forces post in Djibouti, on the Horn of Africa. They landed in Camp Lemonnier at night, were secreted into an operations building where they slept through the day and prepared for the mission to be conducted the following night. After a thorough briefing by intelligence officers, they loaded helicopters from the U.S. Army's 160th Special Operations Regiment, otherwise known as the Night Stalkers—the aviation unit known for its ability to fly helicopters fast, at low altitudes and under extremely hostile conditions. They had more balls than all the other pilots in the military and were the SEAL team's life line.

Intel had estimated thirty terrorists, not the fifty Irish counted with Fish's and Swede's numbers combined. Those were the figures they could *see* on the outside of the main building. The emir could have called a meeting of all of his subordinate leaders, and they could be gathered inside the building, plotting their next murderous raid.

The SEAL team was highly outnumbered, and the rebels were well armed, each carrying a semi-automatic rifle with thirty-round banana magazines and spares.

"Count on fifty to seventy rebels. Your call, Gator," Irish spoke softly into his mic.

The leader of their team Remy "Gator" LaDue's voice crackled through Irish's headset. "They have to sleep sometime."

That was the team's cue to wait and watch.

Irish got comfortable, tucked into a bush, his face blackened with camouflage paint, alert but conserving energy for the battle to come.

Slowly, the rebels settled in for the night, many of them lying in the dirt, weapons clutched in their hands.

An hour went by before the door to the target structure made of straw, sticks and mud opened, and men poured out. Ten loaded into nearby trucks and left, others collapsed onto the ground and talked for a few minutes before lying down to sleep. The village grew quiet.

Forty-five minutes later, Gator's voice came through, "Let's do this."

Irish crawled out of the bush, flexed his muscles and moved forward, shifting his finger to the trigger of his specially modified M4A1. His muscles bunched, his control tight on every movement. Surprise was as much a weapon as the rifle in his hands.

Ten yards before he reached the first perimeter guard hunkered against the side of a hut constructed of sticks, with a grass, thatched roof, Irish paused. The hairs on the back of his neck prickled. Something wasn't right. The ground around him was too clean, too clear. He dropped to his haunches and scanned the area. A thin glint of light alerted him to something shiny stretched between two bushes.

"Fuck! The perimeter is wired—" he said into his mic.

As the words left his mouth, a loud explosion ripped through the silence and shook the earth, spitting dirt and rubble into the air.

Irish flattened against the ground, his pulse slamming through his veins. The trip wire hung inches from his nose. The explosion had gone off to the south where

Swede, Big Bird, Gator and Sting Ray were. Someone had tripped the wire.

Every rebel in the village leaped to his feet shouting, guns at the ready. The door to the target structure burst open, and more men ran out into the yard.

"Plan Bravo!" Gator called into Irish's headset.

Irish, Tuck and everyone else opened fire on the rebels in the village, taking out as many as they could to provide cover while Hank and Dustman carried out their part of Plan Bravo. Positioned twenty feet on either side of Irish, the two SEALs, half-hidden in the brush, came to their knees and fired off two high-explosive grenades from the M203A1 grenade launchers attached to their rifles, aiming for the hut at the center of the village. One landed short, the other hit. Both exploded with a bright flash.

Half of the team pulled back, heading for the helicopter pick-up point. Their communications man would have put in a call to the waiting Night Stalkers. The helicopters would be in position when the SEALs reached the appointed landing zone.

They just had to get there.

Irish, Tuck, Swede and Fish would be the last to bug out, providing cover fire for the others.

"Gator was hit," Big Bird said into Irish's headset. "I've got him."

"Get out of here," Tuck said. "We've got your six."

Irish eased away from the village, firing as he went. The chaos of going from sound asleep to fully alert was wearing off the rebels. In full-defense mode, they fired back, strafing the darkness surrounding the village in hope of hitting their attackers.

Hunkering low to the ground, Irish ran, doing his best to hug the shadows of trees and bushes. With the moon shining brightly, the SEALs could see the enemy, but the enemy could see the SEALs as well, especially when they were on the move.

Less than a mile away, the thumping sound of rotors whipping the air gave Irish incentive to pick up the pace. His teammates sounded off as they boarded the helicopters.

After one chopper filled, it left the ground and headed north toward Djibouti.

Irish could see the outline of the other chopper, the blades stirring dust in the air, whipping leaves and grass like an impatient child ready to leave.

"Come on, Irish," Tuck urged.

The words, barely audible over the pounding of his pulse against his eardrums, gave Irish incentive to pick up the pace. Rifle fire erupted behind him, the thunk of bullets hitting the dirt around him was even more compelling. He gave up zigzagging to avoid catching a bullet and ran full out, leaping aboard the helicopter.

He hadn't even gotten in when the aircraft left the ground, rising up into the air. Tuck grabbed him by his gear and dragged him all the way in the fuselage. Irish sat up and turned toward the open door. Even though he was inside, he wasn't safe yet. The door gunners on both sides fired onto the rebels below.

When the chopper was only fifty feet off the ground, a flash of light below made Irish's blood run cold.

The door gunner barely had time to yell, "Incoming!" when the helicopter gave a violent lurch and spun to the left, tilting precariously, losing altitude at an alarming pace. The pilot attempted to compensate and the craft lurched to the right before it hit the ground.

Irish slid across the floor, scrambling for purchase, his hands finding none. He tumbled out the open door, bounced off the skid and fell twenty feet, landing on his back in a pile of rubble of what had once been a hut. Stunned, with the breath knocked out of his lungs and his vision blurring, Irish watched as the helicopter pitched back to the left, flew another half mile, shuddered and crashed to the ground.

His heart banging against his ribs, Irish tried to rise. Pain shot through the back of his head, and he collapsed. Like a candle's flame in the wind, the moonlight snuffed out.

Dr. Claire Boyette hunkered in the shadows of the underbrush half a mile away from the village of Samada, listening to the sounds of gunfire. She prayed the rebels were shooting each other, not the remaining villagers who'd been forced to give up their homes for the rebels' use. Granted it went against her Hippocratic Oath to wish ill health on another human, but she didn't care. Umar and his thugs had done more damage to the nation than any other rebel faction, and they deserved to die a terrible death.

As soon as a lookout spotted Umar's trucks headed their way a week ago, Claire and her Somali counterpart, Dr. Jamo, had gathered as many of the women and children as they could and hidden them in the brush. Rather than just passing through, Umar and his treacherous entourage rumbled into the grass hut village and took over.

Claire and Dr. Jamo had established a small camp a mile and a half away from the village, off the main road and deep in the brush. They set up makeshift tents with the blankets they scavenged when the rebels weren't looking. But the only source for clean water was in the village. They couldn't keep sneaking in and out in the early hours of the morning without being caught.

That was a week ago, and now the rebels had appeared to be quite settled. Until gunfire erupted, and the sounds of men shouting could be heard all the way to where Claire had dared to lay down her head to sleep.

She had Dr. Jamo hurry the women and children deeper into the brush, abandoning their tents to hide behind bushes and trees in case the rebels came their way. Once her charges were well hidden, Claire crept toward the village, staying far enough away she wouldn't catch a stray bullet. She hoped. Her fear was for the welfare of the other villagers who'd been forced to stay and had been sneaking food and water out to the others.

As a medical doctor, she wanted to be nearby to help those injured in the shooting.

As she neared the village, the gunfire increased and the thumping sound of a helicopter's blades churned the air. Rethinking her decision to check out things in the heat of a battle, Claire had started to turn when a helicopter left the ground and flew over the top of her head. From its shape and the guns mounted on each side, she'd bet it was an American Black Hawk. She'd seen enough of them when she'd passed through Camp Lemonnier, before she made her way into Somalia a month ago. Though the aircraft had gone, the thumping sound of rotors hadn't ceased.

Claire leaned around a bush and spotted another chopper in the distance as it rose from the ground and headed her direction.

A flash streaked from the ground nearby and was followed by a loud bang. The aircraft shuddered and the blades dipped to one side.

Claire tensed. Instinct made her duck, even though the helicopter flew well over her head. But not for long. Apparently, the chopper had taken a hit and was going down. As it tipped back the other way something...or someone ...fell to the ground within twenty yards of where Claire hid.

By the shape she could see in the moonlight, it was a man. She rose from her position, and started toward the spot where he'd landed. Before she'd gone five feet, the helicopter crashed into the ground half a mile away with a loud crunching of metal. The blades broke off and sliced through trees.

Claire hunkered low and kept running toward the downed man.

The rebels cheered, loaded into trucks and raced from the village to the fallen aircraft, headlights piercing the darkness.

Flames rose from the crash site and another explosion rocked the ground beneath Claire's feet.

Keeping close to the shadows of trees and bushes, Claire arrived at the spot she thought she'd seen the man fall. At first, all she could make out was the charred remains of a mud and straw building that had long been burned to the ground. Outside the village, it had probably belonged to a shepherd. Now the hut was nothing but a jumble of grass, rocks and sticks.

Claire glanced all around and was about to give up and hide herself when she heard a moan.

The trucks with the rebels would be near her position any minute.

To the side of a large pile of the rubble, lay a dark figure. Claire crouched beside him and checked for a pulse by pressing two fingers to his neck. If she had time, she'd unbuckle his helmet and loosen his bulletproof vest. But she didn't, and he didn't have the time for her to do anything but kick, scrape and rake rocks and bramble over his body, hiding him from view of the rebels, should they pause to check out the remains of the hut.

Claire did the best she could before throwing herself

into the brush behind a large bush. There she lay, breathing as quietly as she could.

Men carrying guns tromped past the burned-out shell of the structure, barely glancing in the direction of the man half-hidden beneath rocks, brush and sticks.

As soon as the men went by, Claire returned to the man in black, aware more rebels would be headed their way. She had to do a better job of hiding the soldier or risk him being discovered.

Irish floated in and out of consciousness. Each time he tried to sit up, pain shot through his head, his vision clouded and he slipped back into an abyss of nothingness. Several times a pale feminine face hovered over his, surrounded by blue-tinged, light-colored hair. Cool fingers pressed to the base of his throat. "Did I die?" he whispered, his voice barely audible.

"Shh." She pressed a slim finger to his lips.

He puckered, kissing the pretty lady's finger. "Are you an angel?" Was it against the rules to kiss an angel? He didn't care.

"You have to be silent," his angel said. "Lie very still." She pushed rocks and brush over his body.

Irish blinked in and out, disturbed that his angel seemed intent on burying him. A stab of pain ripped through his head again, and he winced. "Dead sure hurts a lot."

"You're not dead," she assured him.

Though the SEAL in the back of his mind echoed

death was the easy way out, none of his muscles responded to do anything about it. He lay as still as a dead man, slipping back into the blackness.

On another trip up to consciousness, moonlight barely came to him through the leaves and branches piled on his face. He lay on the hard ground, rocks and bramble digging into his back, his body covered in dirt, branches and grass. The earthy smell of dirt and dried leaves filled his nostrils. Again, he attempted to sit up, but the weight of his own body and the rubble covering him was more than he could lift.

In the back of his mind, he knew there was something he should be doing. A task both dangerous and urgent. If only he could stand, grab his weapon and move. Again, he slipped away, waking only when he felt hands on his chest and legs.

He tried to raise his arm to block the attack, but he couldn't make it move. It was as though a heavy weight had settled over his entire body. He was helpless to move and not conscious enough to protest.

"Lie still," the angel's voice whispered into his ear, her breath warm against his skin.

He blinked open his eyes and stared up into dark pools of indigo. There she was again, the woman who'd visited him before. He wanted to know her name. He opened his mouth to ask, but the pain knifed through his head, and he moaned.

"Shh. You must be quiet, or we'll be caught," his angel whispered.

"Kiss me." His head and body ached, and his vision grew more blurred. "Please."

"If you promise to be quiet."

He blinked once. "SEAL's honor."

She bent and pressed her lips to his.

He smiled, the pain receding for a moment, warmth stealing over him at her touch. She truly was an angel of mercy.

The sounds of footsteps and equipment rattling nearby disturbed the night.

"Lie still," his angel repeated. She covered his face with a branch and disappeared.

If he died now, at least he'd go having been kissed by an angel.

ABOUT THE AUTHOR

ELLE JAMES also writing as MYLA JACKSON is a *New York Times* and *USA Today* Bestselling author of books including cowboys, intrigues and paranormal adventures that keep her readers on the edges of their seats. When she's not at her computer, she's traveling, snow skiing, boating, or riding her ATV, dreaming up new stories. Learn more about Elle James at www.ellejames.com

Website | Facebook | Twitter | GoodReads | Newsletter | BookBub | Amazon

Or visit her alter ego Myla Jackson at mylajackson.com
Website | Facebook | Twitter | Newsletter

Follow Me!
www.ellejames.com
ellejames@ellejames.com

ALSO BY ELLE JAMES

Hellfire in High Heels (#4)

Playing With Fire (#5)

Up in Flames (#6) TBD

Total Meltdown (#7) TBD

Mission: Six

One Intrepid SEAL

Two Dauntless Hearts

Three Courageous Words

Four Relentless Days

Five Ways to Surrender

Six Minutes to Midnight

Hearts & Heroes Series

Wyatt's War (#1)

Mack's Witness (#2)

Ronin's Return (#3)

Sam's Surrender (#4)

Take No Prisoners Series

SEAL's Honor (#1)

SEAL'S Desire (#2)

SEAL's Embrace (#3)

SEAL's Obsession (#4)

SEAL's Proposal (#5)

High Country Hideout (#7)

Clandestine Christmas (#8)

Thunder Horse Series

Hostage to Thunder Horse (#1)

Thunder Horse Heritage (#2)

Thunder Horse Redemption (#3)

Christmas at Thunder Horse Ranch (#4)

Demon Series

Hot Demon Nights (#1)

Demon's Embrace (#2)

Tempting the Demon (#3)

Lords of the Underworld

Witch's Initiation (#1)

Witch's Seduction (#2)

The Witch's Desire (#3)

Possessing the Witch (#4)

Stealth Operations Specialists (SOS)

Nick of Time

Alaskan Fantasy

Blown Away

Warrior's Conquest

Rogues

Enslaved by the Viking Short Story

Conquests

Smokin' Hot Firemen

Love on the Rocks

Protecting the Colton Bride

Heir to Murder

Secret Service Rescue

High Octane Heroes

Haunted

Engaged with the Boss

Cowboy Brigade

Time Raiders: The Whisper

Bundle of Trouble

Killer Body

Operation XOXO

An Unexpected Clue

Baby Bling

Under Suspicion, With Child

Texas-Size Secrets

Cowboy Sanctuary

Lakota Baby

Dakota Meltdown

Beneath the Texas Moon

Printed in Great Britain
by Amazon